ADVANCE PRAISE

When you are denied the right to play in the USA, you are deported to Canada, just like myself! The protagonist in *Long Way Home* seems (no pun intended) to be living the prequel of my life. I too ended up with a lovely girl from Saskatchewan. Always take "The Long Way Home ." This is a great read! The band Supertramp, would love it, the King Eddie Feigner...move it on over!

-Bill "Spaceman" Lee

Long Way Home

Dwayne Brenna

Pocol Press

Punxsutawney, PA

For Ron
On his 89th birthday!
A fellow barnstormer
in a game of life + golf!
Best regards,
Dwayne

POCOL PRESS
Published in the United States of America
by Pocol Press
320 Sutton Street
Punxsutawney, PA 15767
www.pocolpress.com

Publisher's Cataloguing-in-Publication

Names: Brenna, Dwayne, author.
Title: Long way home / Dwayne Brenna.
Description: Punxsutawney, PA: Pocol Press, 2022.
Identifiers: LCCN: 2022932999 | ISBN: 979-8-9852820-2-3
Subjects: LCSH Baseball--History--Fiction. | Baseball players--Fiction. | Saint Louis (Mo.)--Fiction. | Historical fiction. |
BISAC FICTION / Sports | FICTION / Historical / General
Classification: LCC PS3602 .R4491 L66 2022 | DDC 813.6--dc23

Library of Congress Control Number: 2022932999

ACKNOWLEDGEMENTS

The author would like to thank his fellow writer's group members—David Carpenter and David Margoshes—for their many helpful suggestions. He would like to acknowledge and thank the Hambidge Artists' Colony for putting Georgia on his mind and Steve Kettmann and Sarah Ringler, at the Wellstone Center in the Redwoods, for sharing their interest in good writing and good baseball. And, as always, he would especially like to thank his wife Beverley for her willingness to listen to the next chapter and his sons Wilson, Eric, and Connor for their love and support.

For my sons

Table of Contents

1. Prophecy

They waited in a door well at the corner of Wharf and Chestnut. Ray sat, propped against the shiplap of an abandoned tobacco shop, dungarees smudged and thin cotton shirt pasted to his torso in the heat. Spitz crouched beside him and peered out at the street, wondering how things ever went so wrong. And what he had to do to make them right again. In his scrubby duffle bag, propped against a stone wall nearby, was whatever he could call home. A suit of clothes. A thick woolen undershirt. A toothbrush and a comb. A jockstrap and a weathered baseball glove.

Spitz remembered jazz and fast women whenever he came to St. Louis. He'd been here in his salad days, before the railway went bankrupt in '33, before Dizzy Dean and Joe Medwick. The Cardinals weren't so good back then, and Spitz remembered handing them their asses almost every time he'd pitched. The fans were genteel along the baselines and unsophisticated in the outfield bleachers.

Down the street, other men were gathered around a steel girder outside a bar, eating pigs' knuckles, glasses of beer in hand. They mopped their foreheads with dirty white handkerchiefs and whistled at the few women who ventured by. As Spitz watched the drinkers quaffing their cool ale, the old ache returned to his body. His lips were dry as salted fish.

There was anger somewhere in the city. Spitz could hear the tumult of raised voices, the clatter of placards against one another, and the hard thud of boots on brick roadways. The hubbub seemed to be coming closer, reverberating in waves down Chestnut Street. Spitz stepped out of the shade to observe the goings-on. He could see, in the distance, a hundred men marching toward him. The drinking men turned and watched the oncoming protest. "What's goin on?" Spitz asked one of them, a fellow in a button-down collar and pin-striped white trousers.

"Goddamn Trotskyites," the man replied. "Think they're gonna bring communism to this fair land."

Then there was a siren's wail and the throaty voices of automobile engines and a high, shrill whistle, and the protesters broke into a run. Policemen chased them, truncheons drawn. Spitz could see a policeman battering a fallen man, who quickly lost consciousness as other rioters stampeded around him. In a doorway just down the street, he saw three protesters kicking a cop. The man in the pin-striped trousers strolled out into the street and confronted one of the Trotskyites, receiving a punch in the face for his labors. He spat some blood and a couple of teeth onto the brick road and watched as his adversary ran away. The protesters scattered to avoid further punishment, and Spitz could see that they were not demons or spies or criminals. They were young men, just like him, who had fallen on hard times. Maybe they had worked in the brickyards before the brickyards went defunct.

When the protest had passed, Spitz returned to the shade of the doorway, where Ray was still resting against the tobacco shop door. Ray looked at Spitz like a child looks at his father. "Why are people so angry?"

"They jus' need some work to keep 'em outta trouble," Spitz replied.

"Does work keep ya outta trouble?"

"Some work does." Spitz peered down the street, looking for the bus. He wondered if he'd misheard the Preacher on the phone. Corner of Wharf and Chestnut was what he thought the Preacher had said. Not far away, the Mississippi River rolled by, unconcerned with the fate of men.

Ray looked like a boiled owl. "I'm hot, Spitzy." He fanned himself with his cap.

"Why don't you play your harmonica to pass the time?"

"I don't wanna."

"Well, you don't hafta if ya don't wanna. I'm jus' sayin."

"Are we gonna play a game of baseball?"

"Yes, we are."

"Are we gonna give these Cardinals a lickin?"

"I keep tellin ya," Spitz said. "We're gonna drive outta town and play some country teams."

"Is that what the Preacher said?"

"That's what the Preacher said."

"Think I'm gonna like baseball," Ray said, as though he'd never played the game before. It made Spitz want to cry. "Maybe I will play us a song." Ray reached into the breast pocket of his shirt and pulled out a harmonica. He blew into it, high and mighty. Spitz recognized *The Gambler's Blues*. One thing Ray never forgot was how to play the mouth harp.

A ragged fellow and his dog approached them from across the street. The man was wearing a tattered shirt and baggy trousers and worn-out shoes. He had a grey beard and silver hair. The smell of booze and sweat cascaded off him. The dog was a mangy, cockeyed mutt, maybe blind. His hind legs didn't seem to line up with his front. "You play and I'll dance," the man said to Ray. "We'll split the take."

Spitz couldn't tell whether Ray heard the old man or not, but Ray kept blowing into the harp. The ragged fellow placed his felt hat gently on the sidewalk and began to dance. He started out with some soft shoe but, as the harmonica reached for a crescendo, he leapt into the air and twirled, clicking the heels of his weathered shoes before lightly touching down. The dog sat, guarding the hat, ears alert, his eyes trained on his master, enjoying the spectacle. The old man could dance. He looked to be about seventy, but he danced like a twenty-year-old. He leapt again, so high that Spitz could hardly credit his own eyes. The old man chuckled at Spitz's amazement, and the dance continued. A few passersby stopped and watched. They dropped nickels and dimes in the hat before moving on.

When the song and dance ended, the old man spread the coins on the sidewalk and divvied up the take. He placed fifty-five cents in Ray's hand. Then he tipped his hat and headed down the street, the dog sidewinding along with him.

Spitz called after the old man. "What's yer name?"

The old fellow stopped and turned. "Folks call me Bojangles."

"You sure can dance," Spitz said back.

Warming to the compliment, Bojangles took a few steps toward Spitz. "Used to dance for a livin," he said, "at minstrel shows and carnivals and such. Just one of my many talents."

"Oh?" Spitz said. "What other talents do you have?"

"I can also tell yer fortune," the old man replied. "Have ya got two bits?"

"Not for a fortune teller, I don't."

Bojangles cleared his throat, sizing up Spitz as a conman sizes up his mark. "Have ya got a dime?"

Spitz didn't believe in fortune tellers, but he thought to humor the old man. "Guess I could spare a dime."

"Hold out yer hands," Bojangles said.

Spitz did as he was told, and the old man grasped his wrists with long bony fingers. It felt to Spitz like an electric current was suddenly jerking through him. The old man's eyes were closed. "I see you goin on an odyssey," he said in a sing-songy voice. "You will encounter many wondrous thangs. A fella high up on a flagpole. A plague of locusts. A house of dreams. A talking beaver. A woman and a watch. A man who means you good and a man who means you ill."

Bojangles let go of Spitz's wrist and looked at him with the eyes of age. Spitz stared back at him. "You could see all that?"

"All that and more," the old man said, "but some of it yer gonna haff to find out on yer own." He chuckled again, turned gracefully on one heel, and headed down the street. The mangy hound followed. The old man jumped and twirled and clicked his heels as he danced his way through the barroom door.

It wasn't more than an hour later when the bus pulled up, an elderly contraption, brush-painted blue, with the logo "Appalachian All-Stars" painted on the side in bright orange letters. Probably an old city bus from Memphis or Atlanta or somewhere, it was a boxy affair with a blank street destination sign over the windshield and doors at front and rear. The tires were bulging and worn. Between the headlights, a bug-filled square radiator hissed and steamed. At least there were lots of windows, some of them cracked and stained by stones and time, on all sides of the bus. The front door creaked open, and the Preacher was sitting in the driver's seat, a tidy man with grey curly hair pasted low to his head. Spitz remembered playing against him once, at the end of the Preacher's career and the beginning of his own. The Preacher still had the same gnarled fingers, but now they were wrapped around the bus' steering wheel instead of around a piece of hickory. "The last of the exiled Samaritans," the Preacher announced, as Spitz and Ray grabbed their duffle bags and climbed the narrow steps. "And now the holy order is complete."

From the front of the bus, Spitz surveyed the rest of the Preacher's crew. He recognized a few of them as the Preacher had promised he would. Mervin White Calf sat a few rows back. Spitz had played with him in Boston. Rube Larson sat behind White Calf, looking as rangy and unpredictable as Spitz remembered him, back in the day. He wondered how long Rube would last with the Preacher. Rube had never lasted long with any manager. Two rows behind Rube, sitting aloof from the rest, was Fast Eddie Kramer, who'd thrown the World Series in 1929. They all had a past, Spitz knew; they all had to atone for something.

The rest of the players Spitz didn't recognize. There was a midget riding shotgun right behind the Preacher. On the other side of the aisle sat a Black fellow. Spitz couldn't be sure, but he thought the fellow might be Clarence Harms, who'd played right field for the Homestead Greys a few years back. And behind the Black guy sat, of all things, a woman. She was pretty and well-dressed. Spitz wondered if maybe she was somebody's girlfriend. But who would bring a girlfriend on a barnstorming tour like this?

Spitz and Ray claimed two ragged seats near the back of the bus and across from one another. Ray played his harmonica as the bus rumbled down the street. He started with "Brother Can You Spare a Dime?" and graduated to "Ain't We Got Fun?" They left the environs of the city and sped into the dustbowl, heading north. Spitz sat there, looking out his dirty window, wondering what the hell he'd gotten himself into.

2. Brown

It was early June and everything was brown. The grass was brown. The sky was brown. The houses, smeared with dust, were brown. The faces of the travelling folk who walked alongside the road were brown, made so by the wind and inveterate sun. The horses and the dogs were brown.

There wasn't a lot of traffic on the road. No one could afford the price of gasoline except travelling baseball teams who brought the purity of the game into towns sullied with sacrifice and survival. Looking out the back window of the bus, Spitz could see a lonesome black sedan a quarter mile behind them. It was a newer model, one of them Fords with the V8 engine that could go faster than any police car. The sedan maintained a steady pace in the wake of the bus; when the bus slowed, the sedan slowed. Spitz wondered why the driver of that sedan might want to ride in a cloud of dust rather than gunning his engine, passing, and driving on ahead where the air was cleaner.

They'd just crossed the state line into Iowa when the bus' shortcomings became apparent. Spitz heard a pop that reminded him of a jug of wine bursting from over-fermentation. The bus swerved and skidded, and then there was the sound of rubber slapping metal. Somehow the Preacher managed to avoid careening into a ditch. He slammed on the brakes and the bus creaked to a stop. "Looks like we got us a flat tire," he announced. Spitz volunteered to lend a hand.

Standing on the side of the road in that raging heat, Spitz and the Preacher perused the damaged tire. It was beyond repair, shredded and thin as paper. "Where'd you pick up this big boat?" Spitz asked the Preacher.

The black sedan slowed and crept by them. The occupants of the car, two men, gave them the once-over as they drove past.

"Got a hell of a deal in Kansas City."

"They didn't pay you to take this junkheap off their hands?"

The Preacher had to laugh.

Together they inspected the spare tire that was mounted behind the front fender on one side of the vehicle. The tire was threadbare and bulging; it looked only marginally better than the tire it was about to replace. They found a jack and a tire wrench and were getting set to lift the bus off the ground when the black sedan pulled up again, this time from the opposite direction. The driver opened his door and stepped out of the vehicle. He sported shiny leather shoes, and he was not dressed for the weather. He wore a three-piece woolen suit and a high collared button-down shirt. As he came closer, Spitz could see that he was short and heavy set, with a scar across one cheek that looked like a joker's smile. "You fellas need any help?" the man asked.

"Looks like we got it figgered out," the Preacher replied, "but thanks fer offerin."

Spitz pumped on the jack, raising, by notches, the rear end of the bus. The Preacher pried on the lug nuts with his tire iron. The nuts were rusted, practically seized to the bolts, but with a little determination and a lot of grunting, they came loose.

"Appalachian All-Stars," the short man read off the side of the bus. "You baseball players?"

The Preacher paused in his exertions. "That we are."

"I only know about one ball player," the man said, sounding like a fan. "Fella by the name of Fast Eddie Kramer. Ever heard of him?"

"Heard of him?" the Preacher replied. "He's on this bus."

"Maybe I'll come and watch you play," the short fellow said. "When's your next game?"

"Tomorrow night in Des Moines," the Preacher told him. "We'd be happy to have your patronage."

The man got back in his car and sped off ahead as Spitz and the Preacher mounted the spare tire on the bus' rear axle. "Nice fella," the Preacher remarked. "Not every man's willin to help a weary traveler in this day and age."

Des Moines was hotter than the hubs, but Spitz liked it hot. His arm felt better in the summer heat, less likely to cartwheel off his shoulder and tumble through the air toward first base with the ball. He had no idea how the game might proceed with that forlorn crew of players the Preacher had signed. He didn't expect the best.

He had a chance to confer with White Calf while he was putting on his cleats. "How'd you git talked into this?" he asked.

"I heard they was drivin up near the Six Grandfathers," he said, "so I decided to tag along."

"The Six Grandfathers?"

"Black Hills is what the white folks call 'em," White Calf said. "That's where I was born."

When the team began warming up in right field, the lady who had been sitting in front of Spitz on the bus walked out onto the field and warmed up with them. She was throwing long-toss with the midget, and both of them looked like they knew their way around a ball diamond. Spitz sidled over. "Name's Tom," he said. "Everybody calls me Spitz."

The midget spoke up first, his voice like a squeaky wheel. "We know who you are," he said. "I'm Everett, but the Preacher puts me in the lineup as the Child Prodigy."

The lady shook his hand. "I'm Betty Jane Lindblom." Her grip was surprisingly strong.

Spitz was beginning to get a clearer picture of what the Preacher had in mind. He'd amassed a team of novelty players to shock and delight opposing teams and their fans. This was more about entertainment than baseball. In his telephone call a month earlier, the Preacher had been anything but clear. "We're goin on an all-star tour," he'd said, "all the way from Des Moines through Iowa and Wyoming and the northern states and then up into Canada. It'll be mostly small-town ball against a bunch of hicks and bushers with a couple of city teams thrown in for good measure. We'll always win, of course. The team gits an appearance fee of twenty-five bucks per game and half the gate, out of which each player gits a crisp five-dollar bill."

"Who else is comin along?" Spitz had asked.

"Hasn't been entirely decided yet," the Preacher had replied, "but there'll be guys you know. Fast Eddie. White Calf. Guys like that."

"And Ray," Spitz had said.

"And Ray," the Preacher had replied, but he hadn't sounded too sure.

As the warmup continued, Spitz noticed a crew of workers planting trees behind the low home run fence. He strolled over and talked to them. They seemed like ordinary citizens, some of them dressed too fancifully for the kind of work they were doing, others in coveralls and boots. "You folks landscapers?" he asked one of the men, a string bean elderly fellow in a suit coat and a poor boy cap.

The man stopped in his exertions and leaned on a shovel. "Just part of the water works program."

"Water works program? What's that?"

"If ya can't pay yer water bill," the old man said, "the city gives you a chance to work it out."

"I guess ya got to have water," Spitz replied.

"Pretty hard to live without it." A supervisor caught the old man's eye, and he went back to work, digging a hole to plant a tree in.

Spitz returned to the warmup, readying himself for the game. It felt good to throw the ball again. It felt like he was preparing for the ancient ritual of the hunt, practicing to down a deer or a bear with a deftly hurled projectile. He played soft toss with Ray, who remembered well enough how to receive and throw a ball although his movements were jerky and mechanical. The Preacher came over and asked him, confidentially, if Ray was fit to play. "He's fit to play long as he wants to play," Spitz replied. "That was the deal. If he doesn't play, I don't play either."

The Preacher had little choice but to honor the original deal he'd made with Spitz. "But you know as well as I do," the Preacher said, "that the ball has a way of finding the one guy on the diamond who doesn't know how to play it."

Across the field, the home team looked spiffy in their laundered white uniforms. They ran drills—the kind of drills they taught you in the minor leagues—with machine-like efficiency. From where he stood, Spitz could see that they were playing at being baseball players rather than playing baseball. They looked good, but they were all about how good they looked. Normally, such a squad would be easy to beat, but Spitz was also concerned with the makeup of his own team.

By seven o'clock, a crowd had gathered in the stands, not a capacity crowd by any means but of a respectable number. The game got underway. In their first at bat, the Black man, who was indeed Clarence Harms, led off with a walk. The Preacher doubled behind him, and Clarence sped home like Tom Longboat at the end of a race. Spitz slapped a single to right field, and White Calf, in the cleanup spot, slammed a towering home run that sent the water works people scattering.

In the bottom half of the first, Spitz's fears about his own team were assuaged. Fast Eddie's fastball was still untouchable, sending batters back to their bench with shell-shocked looks on their faces. Betty Jane Lindblom was a whirling dervish at second base, scooping up groundballs and tossing them breezily to first. In right field, Ray looked tentative, like he didn't know which way he should be facing but, with Eddie pitching, nothing was hit to him anyway. For his part, Spitz settled in at shortstop, remembering how he'd played there in school before the major leagues turned him into a pitcher. He charged the first ground ball he saw, bobbled it, but threw the Des Moines runner out with a bee bee right at Rube, who was playing first base. After that, Spitz remembered the importance of footwork, how the player and the bouncing ball created a kind of dance. Once he was in a rhythm with the ball, everything began to click.

The rest of the game was a yawner. The home team made only weak contact, or no contact at all, with the ball. Clarence stole bases like he owned them. White Calf stroked homer after homer. The Child Prodigy crowded the plate bravely and patiently while the opposing pitcher searched for his miniscule strike zone. He was five-for-five in walks, and the Appalachian All-Stars defeated the boys from Des Moines 22-0.

As the game ended, Spitz noticed that the scar-faced man who had offered them help on the highway was sitting with his crony in the stands behind the plate. He came down to the backstop and congratulated Spitz and the Preacher. "You sure can play," he said. "Where are you playin next?"

"Omaha," the Preacher told him, "and then we're headin north."

The scar-faced man grinned at the Preacher, but his eyes were trained on Fast Eddie, who was icing his elbow on the bench. "Me and my friend are on a little road trip ourselves," he said. "Maybe we'll catch up with you somewhere along the way."

"That'd be grand," the Preacher replied. "We're always happy to see a few friendly faces in the stands."

The Preacher reckoned that not every town along the way would have a decent hotel, but he knew Des Moines was rife with them. As the sun drooped in the west, the Preacher steered the team bus down Locust Street to a hotel called the Savery. It was a grand building, smack in the middle of the city. "We won't be able to afford this kind of accommodation every night of this tour," he announced, "but I figger team management will offer a special treat whilst we can still afford to pay."

He went inside and conferred with a fellow at the registration desk. Spitz saw from the bus that the Preacher was wheeling and dealing. Fifteen minutes later, the Preacher was back on the bus. "I got first-class rooms fer all of you," he crowed. "Come on in and enjoy."

As the players filed through the lobby to the stairs, the fellow at the registration desk called the Preacher over one more time. "You got a Black fella on your team?" he asked in a whisper.

"What of it?"

"He can't stay here."

"Can't stay here?" the Preacher fairly shouted. "We're north of the Mason-Dixon, ain't we?"

The fellow bent low and close to the Preacher. "Please don't make a commotion, sir. We run a respectable establishment."

But the Preacher did make a commotion, and the rest of the team stopped in their tracks near the stairwell. "You're tellin me that all my players can't stay here," he shouted, "and you want me not to make a commotion?"

"I'm telling you, sir, that just one of your players can't stay here," the fellow said, confidentially. "I'd be happy to phone over to Buxton and book him a room, if that works for you."

"No, it doesn't work for me!" the Preacher continued. He turned to his teammates. "We're outta here," he said. "Ain't gonna stay in a shit-hole like this." He kicked a wicker garbage can across the lobby floor on his way out. The rest of the team followed him back to the bus.

The Preacher sat in the driver's seat and stared out the windshield at the skyline of Des Moines. It was a city full of wealth, with new buildings going up even during a depression. The street in front of him was paved with asphalt. He turned to the rest of the players. "Looks like we're sleepin on the bus after all," he said. "I've got some woolen blankets at the back. You can each grab one, if you like."

Fast Eddie was the first to speak up. "Why don't we just try another hotel?"

The Preacher nipped that suggestion in the bud. "If ya hear that sentiment at one hotel, yer gonna hear it at all of them."

"Well, I think we should try," Eddie said.

"I ain't up fer no more shit and abuse," the Preacher argued. "We'll sleep on the bus tonight."

Clarence spoke up. He didn't sound angry or surprised, just sad. "T'ain't no need fer the rest of you to suffer," he said. "Go on back inside. I'll be fine out here."

"That ain't the way this team operates," the Preacher snarled. "On this team, no one's better than the next guy."

As he was gathering blankets for himself and Ray, Spitz reflected on the sudden change from royal accommodation to a more upright sleep. The Preacher was an emotional man, as Spitz knew, but also a wily one. Was it possible that he was using this one desk clerk's refusal as a justification to save accommodation money for the rest of the tour? It was more than possible, Spitz thought. Perhaps it was even likely.

They slept that night on the bus in an alley behind an apartment building. Spitz looked out his window at the latticework of fire escapes that crawled up the back of the neighboring buildings, and then he dozed off. It was an uncomfortable sleep, half sitting, half lying down. He would have preferred a grass bed under a magnolia tree, but there was no grass in sight. Prone to insomnia even at the best of times, Spitz found himself wide awake before the sun came up. He checked his prized pocket watch, a beautiful ornament that Gwendolyn had given him back in Georgia before the times got tough. It wasn't yet 4.30. The other inhabitants of the bus were still asleep. Ray was snoring softly, a woolen army blanket pulled over his head as if to fend off ghosts.

Glancing out the dirty window, Spitz saw, or thought he saw, a flickering light emanating from beneath a grey tarp that covered some rough lumber at a construction site down the alley. A gentle breeze blew up the corner of the tarp every once in a while and Spitz saw, or thought he saw, a bare foot and a trouser leg. Was a person hiding under the tarp? Was he seeking shelter? Or was he dead under there, one of the countless victims of these hard times?

Silently Spitz picked his way down the aisle and pushed open the door. He walked slow and cautious toward the construction site. The wind blew up again as Spitz got closer, and he could see not just the foot and the leg of the man but the torso and one arm, as well. The man was wearing an old-fashioned suit made incongruously of white linen. Spitz stood beside a sawhorse that supported one end of the tarp. "Everything okay in there?" he asked in a whisper. There was no answer, just a rustling as the man changed his position under the tarp and a mechanical click like the lid of a tobacco can closing. Spitz knelt and peered under the tarp. "You okay?" he said again.

The man was turned away from him, but Spitz could see that he was aged. His feet were yellow, almost jaundiced, the way old men's feet get, skin tight as parchment and almost transparent. His hair was white and curly. Spitz could see the outline of a bushy moustache in the fellow's profile. The old man seemed to ignore Spitz, as if ignoring would make him go away. He muttered a word that sounded to Spitz like "hope" or "hole" or something.

"Need any help?" Spitz asked him.

The old man turned to him, at last, and Spitz could see that his eyes were red-hot coals. Tears of lava streamed down the old man's face, burning into his cheeks like acid. "Home," he said, more clearly now. He produced a Smith and Wesson from the folds of his white suit coat and aimed it at Spitz's forehead. "Home," he said again.

When he woke up later that morning, Spitz was lying beside the sawhorse in the vacant construction site. The Preacher was standing over him. "What the hell are you doin out here?" he asked.

The sun had risen behind the Preacher's head, almost too bright to countenance. Spitz looked around, but there was no sign of the old man. He squinted at the Preacher. "Musta sleep-walked."

"Well, let's get you back on the bus." The Preacher reached out a gnarly hand and helped Spitz to his feet. "We gotta be in Omaha by six o'clock."

3. Flat Land

It was mostly flat land west of the Des Moines River. They passed farmsteads where the topsoil had blown clear away, where there was nothing left but a base of coarse sand. Some of the unpainted farmhouses were abandoned. Others were inhabited but only barely; whoever occupied those homes were ghosts of their former selves.

Two hours west of Des Moines, on a barren stretch of gravel, the radiator hose burst, popped like a birthday balloon. Steam rose from the engine compartment in a great cloud. The Preacher pulled over to the side of the road, got out of the bus, and lifted the creaky hood. Happy for the opportunity to stretch their legs, the rest of the team disembarked as well. Fanning away the steam with his fedora, the Preacher told his flock not to worry. "Clarence can fix this," he assured them. "There ain't nothin Clarence can't do with a roll of trainer's tape and a little know-how. But we're gonna need some water."

Spitz surveyed the landscape in all four directions. There wasn't a body of water—not a slough or a creek or a dugout—anywhere in sight. He spied a tarpaper shack down the road a way and saw a windmill rising to meet the sky above the shack. "I'll take a walk down to that farm and see if they can spare a pail of water."

"I'll tag along," said Ray.

The two men arrived at the farmstead fifteen minutes later. There was an eerie stillness about the place, no motion anywhere except for the windmill that groaned in the wind. Spitz knocked at the door of the shack. There was no answer, but Spitz could hear a gramophone record, the scratch of the steel needle against the acetone and the soothing voice. "I found a million-dollar baby in a five and ten cent store," Bing sang loud and clear.

Hearing no other voice, Spitz pushed open the door. "Anybody home?" he asked, but he could already see that there was somebody home. She was sitting at a rough wooden table, wearing a hot winter coat over her thin farm wife's work dress, staring out a window at the god-forsaken prairie, an angular, gaunt woman of indeterminate age. She might have been twenty-five or she might have been fifty. Spitz couldn't find a number in her washed-out face and her lifeless hair. He could only surmise that something was terribly wrong. "Pardon me, ma'am," he said. "We were just wonderin if we could borrow a pail of water."

The woman maintained her gaze through the window at a stretch of cropless prairie. Her voice was lifeless as her demeanor. "Pump's still workin," she said in a monotone. "You can find a pail in the barn." In front of her on the table was a bowl of crusted sugar that was crawling with something. Spitz took a closer look. Pale canker worms were crawling up the sides of the bowl. Having eaten most of the sugar, they were dropping themselves onto the table in search of more food.

As they strode across the yard, Spitz could see that the barn door was part way open. There was no livestock to speak of in the corral beside the barn. Something was not right. "You wait over there by the pump," he said to Ray. "I'll get us a pail."

He approached the barn with apprehension. Standing in the doorway, Spitz peered into the darkness, tiny rays of light shooting in like bullets from cracks and nail holes. Something was suspended from a rafter, perhaps the carcass of an animal or a sack of wheat. As he entered, he saw more clearly, in the dusty gloom, the lifeless body of a man dangling from a length of thick hemp rope. The man's face was black and bloated with long death. Flies and birds had done their worst. There was something pathetic about the man's mortality and the greasy coveralls he was still wearing. He was beyond help. Spitz saw two empty ten-gallon pails that had been set neatly against the railing of a stall, almost as though they were the man's last will and testament. He picked up the pails and hurried out of the barn.

Ray was standing beside the pump, waiting, as he had been told to do. He was squinting across the endless horizon when Spitz returned. "Nothing of everything," he muttered. Sometimes Ray could be pretty philosophical. It took some vigorous pumping, but the well eventually produced water, not the clear stuff you'd want to drink but some dark red concoction that looked like a mixture of water and blood. "That's some nasty lookin juice right there," Ray said, and he was right.

"Just so long as it's wet." It was like pumping gravel through a straw, but eventually Spitz managed to fill the two pails. He directed Ray to carry them back to the bus. "Don't spill any of it."

"I won't spill none," Ray said, walking away like a man on a tightrope, the two pails balancing one another, careful as you please.

"And tell the Preacher to come pick me up when he's ready," Spitz hollered after him.

When Ray had gone, Spitz found a spade leaning against the corral and set about digging a hole behind the barn. The sand was hard and packed back there, and Spitz could only muster a four-by-six grave, three feet deep. He reckoned that would be deep enough to keep the coyotes from despoiling the corpse. Cutting the hanged man down with a pocketknife, Spitz dragged him, as best he could, to the grave. He covered the man with a mound of sand and left the shovel standing in the burial mound as a marker. The thought of saying some holy words crossed his mind, but he didn't think he had the right to say them.

The bus was waiting at the end of the dirt approach by the time Spitz was finished. He flashed a time-out signal at the Preacher and made one last trip back to the house. The gaunt lady was still sitting at her scratched wooden table, staring at the empty fields. Canker worms were crawling on her woolen winter coat now, making their way upward toward her face. The gramophone had ceased blaring; there was only the fingernails-on-chalkboard sound of the needle skipping on the record.

"I buried him," Spitz said.

The woman didn't look at him. "I s'pose he needed buryin." Her voice was dull and emotionless.

Spitz stood there looking at her for some time, wondering what he could do to help. "I see the rhubarb still grows beside the house," he said at last. "There's some good eatin if you boil it up." He closed the door behind him and walked back to the bus.

They arrived in Omaha in good time, stopping at a roadside diner on the way to the ballpark. The players had to pay for their own meals—that was the deal—so Spitz chose carefully for himself and Ray. "We'll have the liver and onions," he told the snarly waitress. Spitz wasn't a fan of liver and onions, but beggars could not be choosers, and Ray seemed happy with whatever was put before him.

At the entrance to the ballpark sat a man atop a flagpole. It was hard to tell from the ground, but the man looked to be in a state of pure relaxation. He had erected a platform three feet below the flagpole's tip, and he perched up there on a wooden chair, surrounded by gunny sacks and water jugs. There was a tin pot up there, and a grey woolen blanket for the man to cover himself while he did his business. He had a puppy in his lap, a frightened looking mongrel that he attempted to pacify with petting and with words. A lady on the ground supported the flagpole sitter by hoisting a picnic basket up a long rope that was attached to a pulley. The sitter ate and fed his dog out of the same basket. There was a rough cardboard sign at the base of the pole. "Thirteen days," it read, "and still going strong." Beside the sign, there was an open suitcase, a handful of loose change its only contents. Spitz thought the man had a sweet scam going; it was free room and board for doing sweet zippity-doo.

Rube must have thought it was a pretty good scam too. He began to shinny up the flagpole, much to the consternation of the man on top. "Stop that!" the sitter yelled. "You'll snap this pole in two." Rube was in no mood to listen. He'd spied the puppy up there, and Rube loved puppies. He loved everything about them.

"I'm a-comin up," Rube hollered back. "Don't care what you say."

The sitter tucked the puppy down inside his shirt and grasped the sides of his chair while the flagpole shuddered and swayed with the weight of Rube's big body. Down below, the people gathered, expecting a catastrophe. Rube shinnied up like the farm boy he was, twisting his sturdy legs around the pole. By the time he reached the top, the pole was listing heavily to one side. Fearing for his life, the sitter stood on his chair and leaned in the opposite direction.

Spitz and the Preacher listened near the bottom of the pole, and they could make out some of the conversation.

"Mind if I look at yer puppy?" Rube asked.

The sitter hesitated but then proffered the unhappy pooch. "Sure," he said. "Give him a good once over."

Clinging to the pole with one hand, Rube used the other to scratch the base of the dog's neck. The dog seemed to take to Rube, licking his forearm while the scratching took place. "This hound's ascared of heights," Rube said to the flagpole sitter.

"I'm teachin him not to be."

"Some things dogs ain't meant to learn," Rube replied, looking stink-eyed at the man, "and climbin flagpoles is one of 'em."

They remained like that, in mid-air, the flagpole sitter, the dog, and Rube, for fifteen or twenty minutes. Finally, the Preacher, standing down below with the others in the crowd, yelled up at them. "Rube, git down here. We got a ball game to play and yer startin."

Rube looked up at the sitter. "Mind if I give this pooch to yer lady-friend down there?"

"Then I got nothin here to keep me company," the man protested.

The pole tilted mightily as Rube shifted his weight. "A scared dog ain't no kind of company."

"Okay, okay," the sitter blurted. "You can take him down."

Rube held the animal under one arm and slid slowly down the pole. When he reached the bottom, he handed the whimpering pooch to the lady. "You take good care of this pup," Rube said, "and he'll take care of you."

The Omaha team was warmed up and ready to go by the time the All-Stars arrived on the field. Their manager strolled over as the Preacher was filling out his lineup card. He was a corpulent fellow with a big voice. "I thought you said this was a team of ex-major leaguers?"

"It is," said the Preacher. "I'm an ex-major leaguer. That's Fast Eddie Kramer out there. And Spitz McKague."

"Mmmmhmmm." The manager squinted at him. "And you also got a midget out there. And a lady."

"That's to give your guys a fightin chance," the Preacher said.

The manager shook his fat head. "We can deal with the midget," he said at last, "but we ain't gonna play against no female."

"She's a damn good second baseman!"

"We ain't gonna play against her," the manager repeated. "And that's that."

The Preacher stood his ground. "Well, if ya ain't gonna play against her, we ain't gonna play."

"Fair enough." The manager called his players in from the field.

"Just hold on one cotton-pickin minute," the Preacher shouted. "We got an appearance fee comin to us."

The manager didn't even bother to look at him. "Ain't no appearance fee if ya don't play the game."

Looking up into the stands at the five hundred or so fans who were in attendance, the Preacher began to lose his resolve. He knew, from his army days, that discretion was the better part. "We can't just leave these spectators high and dry," he argued. "They paid good money to be here."

"They paid good money," the other manager shouted back, "but not to watch a ladies' softball player."

Spitz looked on. He surmised that the Preacher was performing a quick calculation, in his head, of the money he stood to lose. Five hundred fans, at twenty-five cents a fan, was a hundred and twenty dollars. And there was also the appearance fee. That would add up to a hundred and forty-five dollars. "Okay," the Preacher shouted at the other manager, "we'll put her on the bench."

"I don't want her on the diamond."

"Okay then," the Preacher said, "if that's the way you're gonna be." He walked back to the visitors' bench like a turkey picking his way through a farmyard on Thanksgiving Day. Betty, who'd heard the entire conversation, was sitting primly at the far end of the bench. She hadn't bothered to put her cleats on. The Preacher stood ten feet in front of her. "They ain't gonna play if yer on the team."

"But I am on the team," Betty said, looking demure in her skirt and bloomers. "You hired me."

"I'm givin you the day off."

"I don't want the day off."

"Yeah, well, I'm givin it to ya."

"With pay?"

The Preacher was doubly exasperated. "Yes, with pay."

Betty picked up her cleats and slung them over her shoulder. She walked toward the exit to the parking lot. "I think it's cruddy," she shouted back at the Preacher, "that you'd stand up for Clarence, back there at the hotel, and not for me."

"Do you also think it's cruddy not to git paid?" the Preacher replied.

Betty didn't grace his question with an answer. "If you need me," she said, "I'll be in a downtown bar, having a gin and tonic."

Before the game started, as the umpire was explaining ground rules, the Omaha manager asked for a clarification of what happens when a team fields less than nine players. "You got some gall," the Preacher said, kicking at the shale behind home plate, "bringin that up after you've refused to play against our second baseman."

The Omaha manager looked pig-eyed at the Preacher. "Rules is rules."

"House rules here apply," the umpire cut in. "If a team fields less than nine players, they forfeit an out every ninth at bat."

It was a close game after that, too close for comfort, in Spitz's opinion. Rube was not in his best form, out on the mound. He seemed distracted by the flagpole sitter in the parking lot and by the fate of the dog he'd rescued. A fire engine went screaming by, in the third inning, and Rube followed it with his eyes all the way to a tenement house that was billowing smoke. On the bench between innings, he chatted up some young girls who'd taken residence along the first baseline. "I dunno what yer problem is tonight," the Preacher said, "but you better find a way to git yer mind back into this game."

To top it off, Omaha had one good pitcher and one good hitter. The pitcher, a little guy with his hat set at a cocky angle, threw hard but none too accurately. He struck out Spitz in his first at bat and then drilled him in the kidney in the second round. Through fear and intimidation, the Omaha kid was able to keep the score close. The hitter was a broad fellow, a left-handed batter with an ass two axe handles wide. He picked up early on Rube's slurve ball, slamming it into the seats behind the home run fence. In the middle of the fourth inning, the Preacher informed Rube that they weren't going to pitch to the broad-beamed fellow anymore.

"Not gonna pitch to him?" Rube said.

"We'll walk him and pitch to the skinny guy that comes up after."

They proceeded in that fashion for the remainder of the game, purposely walking the fellow twice. With each base-on-balls, the big-assed hitter grew more impatient and the Omaha fans grew angrier, shouting derision at Rube and the whole damn team. The All-Stars were leading 3-2 in the bottom of the ninth. Rube was put off his game by the spectators' jeering. He managed to induce two weak grounders which were turned into outs. Then he walked the next two batters. The big-assed Omaha hitter proceeded to the plate. Expecting to be walked a third time, he'd decided to make a show of it, setting himself up in the right-handed batter's box instead of the left. Rube threw him a pitch a foot outside, and the hitter watched as it sailed by him for a ball.

The Preacher called time. He walked out to the mound, and he and Rube and the rest of the infield had a conference. "I don't think this guy is a switch-hitter," the Preacher said.

"What if he is?" Rube asked.

"Then he pounds one into the seats, and we lose the game."

"He looks pretty comfortable wherever he stands," Spitz said.

The Preacher looked back at the Omaha hitter, who was taking a few right-handed practice swings. "I got a hunch he isn't. Let's pitch to the big bastard."

When he was set up again behind the plate, the Preacher squatted and flashed one finger. Rube sent a fastball down the middle, and the hitter watched incredulously.

"Strike!" the umpire said.

The next pitch was a curve. The Omaha batter swung mightily but came up empty.

"Strike two!" exclaimed the ump.

The big-assed fellow backed out of the batter's box and cogitated for a moment. Realizing that he was going to be pitched to, he circled around behind the umpire into the left-handed batter's box.

The Preacher called time again. Not bothering to rise out of his squat, he turned to the umpire. "There's no way a hitter can do that, is there? Bat from two sides of the plate in the same at bat?"

The umpire walked back to the screen and pulled from his back pocket Albert Spalding's *Book of Baseball Rules*. He thumbed through the worn pages until he got to the part about batters' boxes. Reading as quickly as he could, he found the rule and then returned to his place behind the Preacher. "He's right," the umpire said to the Omaha hitter. "You can't bat from two sides of the plate in the same at bat."

There was a general commotion from the Omaha bench at this utterance, and the hometown manager walked out on to the field. "That ain't in the spirit of the game!" he shouted.

The Preacher looked at him cooly. "Rules is rules," he said. "I think I've heard that somewhere before."

White hot with anger, the fans stood up, fists clenched, yelling at the Preacher and the ump. The Omaha hitter shook his head and returned to the right-handed batter's box. He crouched low, concentrating hard, willing himself to learn the art of right-handed hitting in an instant. Rube wound up and delivered the pitch, a hard, late-breaking curveball. The hitter shifted his considerable weight and swung mightily, but the ball sailed past him and into the Preacher's pancake mitt. "Stee-rike three!" the umpire shouted.

The fans were livid. Shouts of "Kill the umpire!" filled the air. Not bothering to change out of his equipment, the umpire walked briskly to the parking lot, got into his automobile, and drove away. Spitz and the All-Stars congratulated each other as oranges and popcorn boxes rained down on the field. The taste of victory was especially sweet when the fans were so entirely unhappy. The home team didn't bother to shake hands.

They waited for Betty in the parking lot until late in the evening. She was clearly making the whole team suffer for the Preacher's lack of support. "I knew she had an attitude," the Preacher said, as they waited, "but I didn't know how much of an attitude it was."

Ray played the harmonica, the Prodigy read Shakespeare, and Rube wondered aloud about the flagpole sitter's dog.

"Forget the fucking dog," the Preacher exhorted him. "Next game we play, you need to focus."

Rube stared out his window at the lonely flagpole sitter, who had his trousers down and was crapping into the tin pail in semi-darkness.

At about one in the morning, a coupe pulled into the parking lot and screeched to a stop. Spitz looked out his window and saw Betty, inside the coupe, conferring closely with the female driver. After a moment, Betty stepped out of the automobile and walked jauntily across the parking lot to the bus. She was still wearing her white baseball skirt and her bloomers.

The Preacher couldn't help commenting as he popped the door open and let Betty into the bus. "It's about time," he muttered. "We bin waitin here since nine o'clock."

Betty flipped her blonde locks out of her eyes. "Next time," she said, "maybe you'll think twice before dropping me from the roster."

4. Perdition

As they drove out of Omaha that night, Spitz saw stately churches and squat brick tenements, wood-frame houses and railroad sidings where homeless people lived. Passing near a confederacy of tents in what had once been a public park, the Preacher shook his head and muttered, "Blessed are the meek, my friends, blessed are the meek." He stopped for gasoline at an all-night station across from the park.

Spitz watched the goings-on across the street, from his window, while a station attendant filled the tank with gas. There was a circle of men, some young, some old, some ragged and some less so, standing at the edge of the encampment. In the middle of the circle were two large men, both shirtless. One was bleeding. Their heads cocked forward and their guards up, they glowered at one another. Both of the pugilists looked exhausted, but the crowd cheered them on. They looked to Spitz like two wild animals, not dogs or bears or tigers but some other breed of animal that hadn't yet been identified. The bleeding man took a run at his foe, and Spitz saw the other man step to one side, his bare fist crashing into the bleeding man's temple. He saw the bleeding man fall and try to get up, saw him get to his feet and fall a second time. The bleeding man was trying to work out the laws of gravity when his foe delivered a boot to the side of his head. He did not get up again. There was a moment of joy and utter sadness in the crowd that surrounded the two pugilists, and Spitz knew the fight was over.

Ray pulled out his harmonica and played a tune called "Ain't Misbehavin." Spitz could feel his teammates relax as the mouth harp wailed. In the seat in front of him, Betty sat up straight and unreasonably happy. Even Eddie, aloof and in his own world, seemed suddenly more comfortable. Ray still had one talent. He could make people happy.

They were riding through the Nebraska farmland when Spitz fished in his pocket for his brass pocket watch. He admired its ornate casing, flowers and vegetation embossed on one side.

He'd lost the chain some months earlier. He held the watch to his ear and listened to its tick tick tick. It reminded him of a beating heart. He imagined the watch's inner workings, gears within gears and cogs within cogs, turn screws and hair springs. The mechanics were too complicated to understand. Life was like that, Spitz thought, gears within gears, too complicated. When men thought, God—if He was still out there and if He still cared—laughed.

Spitz examined the inscription on the back of the watch. "To Tom," it said, "with all my love, Gwendolyn." He pressed the watch to his lips, then listened to it one more time. His life had fallen apart, but there was still hope if Gwendolyn was in the world.

They played in Ogallala that next evening, winning handily behind Fast Eddie's pitching. It was a small crowd and a small take, but the Preacher gladly accepted the appearance fee. They slept in a seedy hotel on the edge of town.

Then they moved on to a smaller town called Perdition on the other side of the Wyoming state line.

Spitz figured that, in most communities, if folks were going to take exception, they were going to take exception to Clarence. Some concerned people would get to asking questions. What was a Black man doing barnstorming around the countryside with a bunch of white men and one white woman? Did they all eat together? Drink from the same water jug? Maybe someone had to share a room with the darkie?

It was different in Wyoming. Mervin White Calf was suddenly the devil everybody feared and hated. As they got set to play, Spitz could see animosity in the faces of the other team. The home side, and the fifty or so fans that had gathered, were riding White Calf from his first at bat. "Hey Comanche," Spitz heard the catcher whisper at him, "how many scalps you got so far today?" The pitch was delivered, a fastball on the outside corner, and White Calf swung nice and easy. From the on-deck circle, Spitz watched as the ball vanished over the centerfield fence. The catcher took off his mask and stared as the ball kept climbing up and up into the warm July evening. White Calf admired it too, standing still at home plate. The burly catcher turned to him and said, "Better run, you fuckin Indian." There wasn't a smile on White Calf's face as he trotted slowly around the bases.

That hick-town catcher was still mumbling by the time Spitz approached the plate. "Your boy is pretty full of hisself," he said as Spitz was digging into the batter's box.

"Has a right to be," Spitz replied, "ex-major leaguer and all." He slapped a single between first and second and scampered down the line.

It went on like that for the rest of the game, and Spitz could tell things were coming to a head. White Calf would step up to the plate, that back catcher would say something, and White Calf would blast a moonshot so hard it probably startled one of them high altitude balloonists that everyone was talking about. By the sixth inning, the crowd of spectators had grown to five hundred or so. It was as if the whole town sensed that a good tar and feathering was about to happen, and they didn't want to miss out on the fun. Local businessmen were there in bowler hats and grey suits, but mostly the crowd consisted of skinny cowboys who'd tethered their horses to a hitching post behind the rickety wooden bleachers. They spat chewing tobacco on the ground like it was sulfuric acid and mumbled to one another every time White Calf strode to the plate. One of them cowboys, blue-eyed and rosy-cheeked, called out in a pleasant voice as White Calf rounded the bases a third time. "I thought we'd sent yer red ass packin fifty years ago," he shouted, "up there in South Dakota." Others in the crowd guffawed as though he'd just told a side-splitter.

In the top of the ninth, Preacher Bentham and his Appalachian All-Stars were winning 15-1. There was nothing left to prove, but that stupid Wyoming catcher thought he had to prove it anyway. He peered up through his mask at White Calf and hissed one or two words. Even standing as close as he was, Spitz couldn't hear what the catcher said. White Calf called time, took one step backwards with that thirty-eight-inch club he called a bat resting on his shoulder, and then he brought the lumber down on the catcher's head. It seemed to happen in slow motion, at least in Spitz's eyes, the burly catcher hissing up at White Calf, the deliberate raising of the hand to call time, the step backwards like he was going to take a walk somewhere and think about all the injustices in his life, and then the arc of the bat as it came down like Thor's hammer on the guy's noggin.

The moment after that was even slower. There was a stillness in the air, the kind of stillness that precedes a summer storm after long hot days. The cowboys stopped their jawing in mid-sentence. Businessmen turned from their wives, drawn away by the soft mesmerizing thud of bat hitting bone. The catcher didn't have far to fall, but he took his time getting there. He looked up at White Calf as much as to ask, "What just happened?" and then his eyes rolled back in his head and he dropped to one knee. The umpire hadn't even lowered his chest guard by the time the hometown catcher fell forward onto the plate. Spitz could see a trail of saliva oozing from the catcher's mouth.

Somebody yelled, "What?"

Then the soft, moist fabric of the dusk was rent with howls of confusion. White Calf didn't stick around. There was but one way out of the ballpark and that was the road through town. Figuring that the team bus would offer little sanctuary against the advance of the locals, White Calf sprinted hard up that road, spraying gravel with his cleats. It took those cowboys a few minutes to untie their horses. Even so, Spitz thought White Calf was a goner. Those good ol' boys would catch up with him, sure as Christ himself was a cowboy, and they weren't gonna be in good humor when they did.

A few of the hometown players dragged their unconscious teammate off the field and rested his sleeping carcass against the backstop. Spitz could tell that the guy was still breathing by the bubble of snot that protruded and receded from one nostril. The rest of the Wyoming boys proceeded on to the field, three of them with a piece of hickory in hand. The Preacher was first to speak up. "Hold on just one cotton-pickin minute," he shouted. "You boys all saw that the feller had it comin, ridin White Calf like he did."

"That don't make no never mind," a big kid with a bowl-cut shouted back. "It's an eye fer an eye in these parts."

The Child Prodigy was digging frantically through the equipment bag as the Perdition boys advanced. The Preacher motioned at the rest of his players to get on the bus. Spitz and some of the others took his advice. The Preacher talked fast. "Consider the Good Book, my friends," he proselytized. "Vengeance is mine, saith the Lord."

Those Wyoming boys just kept coming toward him. They were about to pounce on the Preacher when a gunshot rang out. The Child Prodigy was standing behind the Preacher, wielding a Colt .45 that was twice as long as his arm. "First fool that swings a bat at the holy man," he wheezed, "eats an ounce of ordnance."

The Preacher commenced backing away from the bat wielding Wyoming boys, edging ever closer to the open door of the bus. Before making his exit, he yelled at the coach of the opposing team. "You promised me half the gate."

The other team's coach was standing near his own bench, smoking a cigarette. "You forfeited that when you injured our best catcher," he shouted back.

"Well," said the Preacher, "that ain't very sportin of ya." He leapt on to the bus, and the Child Prodigy leapt on behind him. The infernal contraption started dutifully for a change, with the Preacher at the wheel, and they sped out of the parking lot with a plume of dust behind them.

Some of the cowboys had already fanned out though the town by the time the bus turned down Main Street. It seemed to Spitz that White Calf might be dead by then, but the Preacher sped down an alley to the railway siding that was their emergency reconnoiter point. They stopped and waited near some empty boxcars. There was gunfire in the town. Five minutes passed, maybe more. The gunfire was getting closer. The Preacher slammed the bus into gear and began to edge away. White Calf emerged grim-faced and panting from behind a granary annex and stood in front of the bus' headlights. The Preacher opened the door and White Calf got in, grasping a railing behind one of the seats as the bus jolted along the grassy ridges of the alley. They were half a mile from the town before they realized they were being followed.

Spitz peered out the greasy window at the headlights of the tailing cars and the gun-toting cowboys that rode behind them on palominos and appaloosas. He kept his head low in case one of those cowboys could properly take aim off a galloping horse.

Up at the front of the bus, the Preacher was swearing something terrible and driving for all he was worth, swerving to miss the occasional pothole, banging and grumbling and puddle-jumping along the loose gravel. Past ranches and Indian reservations they sped. The cowboys on their horses were first to disappear in the distance. Then, as they neared the state line, the cars that were tailing them slowed. From his vantage point at the back of the bus, Spitz could see them pulling over in a line that must have stretched a quarter of a mile down the road. He breathed a sigh of relief when he saw by their shifting headlights that the cars were at last turning around and heading back to where they came from.

It was dark by the time they reached the Black Hills, but Spitz could see the outline of the majestic peaks standing like elder statesmen against the sky.

They camped in the Black Hills that night. The Preacher had found a dirt road, off the main thoroughfare, that led into a valley with a creek running through it. Darkness had fallen, almost pitch darkness, no moon in the sky. Betty went down to the side of the creek, stripped off her jersey and washed herself in the cool dark water. The rest of the team were in the bus, readying themselves for sleep, propping equipment bags against windows for use as pillows, unfolding threadbare quilts that mothers or old girlfriends had sewn. They arranged their lanky frames, as best they could, for a mostly upright sleep. Of all the players, Clarence seemed most comfortable with this arrangement. The Child Prodigy was the only one of them who could stretch out fully on a single seat, so he was also set for a good night's sleep.

Spitz checked on Ray, as he always did when turning in. Blowing softly into his harmonica, Ray managed a smile with his eyes to let Spitz know that he was all right. Still not asleep by the time Betty returned to the bus, Spitz heard her pry open the folding door. "God damn, it smells in here," she murmured, mostly to herself, and then she trudged to her seat, pulled a woolen afghan up around her neck, and drifted off. Looking out his window into the darkness, Spitz thought about the moment where everything went off the rails. Was it the moment he was born? Was it the moment he fell in love with the Smoky Mountain girl, when he decided he would lie, steal, and cheat to keep her? Or was it that moment in time, that one pitch he threw before giving up pitching forever, the one nobody could hit. And only he knew the reason why they couldn't.

When daylight broke, Spitz had the feeling that something was awry. He heard the Preacher's wheezing snore. Peering over the back of the seat through crusty eyelids, he saw Ray's head lolled forward, the harmonica no longer in his mouth. Clarence looked peaceful as death, and Betty's hands were clasped, lady-like, under her curls. Spitz heard every bone in his spine popping into place as he straightened up and looked out the window at the coming day.

Standing by the creek, looking due north, was Mervin White Calf. He'd managed to change into his street clothes, and he was looking like he'd never played a game of baseball in his life. He didn't appear to be washing, and he wasn't in a prayerful pose. He was just standing there, looking north. There was a suitcase at his feet.

Sometimes Spitz knew what was going on inside people's minds. It was a gift he had. He could tell that White Calf was about to do something that was irreversible, that would change not only White Calf's life forever but also the lives of everybody on the bus. Spitz decided to intervene. Throwing on his tattered warmup jacket, he sidled down the long corridor to the front of the bus. Gently he pulled the lever that opened the door, looking back to make sure that no one else was stirring. He didn't want to attract unnecessary attention; it was White Calf's decision to make and White Calf's alone.

Walking down to the side of the creek, Spitz came to a stop twenty feet away from White Calf. The creek babbled like a newborn baby. White Calf just kept looking into the distance.

"Nice day," Spitz said softly.

White Calf didn't look at him. "Spitzy," hc murmured. There was great affection in his voice, like Spitzy was the name of his favorite horse.

"It's a beautiful place," Spitz said, "the place where you grew up."

Still concentrating on something in the distance, White Calf replied, "Won't be long before this creek goes dry. Won't be long before the water's no good to drink."

"Are you leavin us?" Spitz asked.

"My people need me."

"Baseball needs you, buddy."

"Baseball's a hard game," White Calf replied.

"Not hard for you."

"Hard for anybody. Specially hard for an Indian."

Spitz followed White Calf's gaze northward and up into the mountains. There, as the sun climbed in the sky, he saw a chiseled face high on a chalky mountain cliff. It was the same face that graced the few greenbacks in his wallet. There was wooden scaffolding around the face, like Nature itself was being rebuilt. The rising sun glinted off that face. Spitz's eyes almost hurt to look at it.

"You see what they done to one of the Grandfathers," White Calf said. He was looking directly at Spitz now.

"I'm sorry" was all that Spitz could muster.

"It ain't yer fault, Spitzy," White Calf said. He grinned and shook his head. "Tell the Preacher I just had to go."

"I'll tell him."

"Love ya, Spitzy," White Calf said. "You're a warrior."

"Love you too."

Spitz and White Calf stood looking at each other for a good long time. They knew their teammates would be waking up in a few minutes. "Let's not git weird about this," White Calf said at last. He picked up his suitcase, turned and headed east, following the creek up into higher ground. The last Spitz saw of him was a shock of black hair heading into the evergreens. Soon White Calf's coloring was lost in the hues of the forest.

5. Chickens

"Fucking hell!" the Preacher exclaimed. "You just let him walk away?"

"Not much I could do," Spitz told him. "He wasn't askin my permission."

"Fucking hell!" the Preacher repeated. "He was our cleanup hitter."

"I know." Spitz was bending down, poking at the campfire with a stick. Salt pork sizzled in a cast iron pan on the grate. Other players straggled off the bus, looking like a badly drawn alphabet with their spines bent by a night of sleeping awkwardly. Ray was down by the creek, blowing high and loud into his mouth harp, greeting the morning, as he always did, with a jaunty anthem.

"Would you please stop that cock-sucking god-awful caterwauling!" the Preacher yelled at him.

Spitz looked at the Preacher steely-eyed. "There's no call for that. He ain't doin nothin but what he always does."

The Preacher stared hard back at Spitz, and they were like a couple of dogs in a blinking contest. "Shithouse mouse," he muttered, averting his gaze at last. "I can't even hear myself think."

Others gathered around the fire, looking for grub. Fast Eddie was rubbing his arm, having pitched eight innings the night before. Betty sat on a rock, warming her well-manicured fingers by the fire. Clarence came off the bus, humming some Memphis blues. The Child Prodigy was right behind him.

"Who died?" Fast Eddie asked.

The Preacher gave him a stink-eyed look.

"Yer standin there lookin like you seen a ghost," Eddie continued.

"I have seen a ghost," the Preacher replied. "I've seen a ghost sure as shit. It was the ghost of White Calf vamoosing outta here."

"White Calf's gone?

"Like shit off a shiny shovel," the Preacher said. "Spitzy here saw him go."

The Child Prodigy turned to Spitz, his words coming out in a machine gun ratatatat. "Why'd he go?"

Spitz shrugged. "Said his people needed him."

"Maybe he was upset about last night."

"Maybe," Eddie said, "but I never knew White Calf to let a little bat swingin incident dampen his enthusiasm."

"Yeah," the Prodigy admitted, "I s'pose that's right."

The Preacher took a walk down to the creek, then turned and walked back again. "We need to have a team meeting." He surveyed his ragtag gang for a moment, his eyes falling stonily upon each player as though they'd all disappointed him beyond measure. "Where's Rube?"

"Went fer a dip in the creek," the Prodigy told him.

"Well, he's half a brick short of a load anyway," the Preacher retorted. "We might as well meet without him."

"Can we git something to eat first?" Clarence said. "I ain't had a bite since suppertime."

The Preacher was going to say something rude but thought better of it. He shook his head. "Yeah, go ahead and eat," he said. "Spitzy's got salt pork in the pan. There's a loaf of bread on the hood of the bus. I need to cool down anyway."

When breakfast was done, they all got back on the bus. Spitz sat by Ray. He shook his head when Ray was about to bring the harmonica to his lips. Rube sat behind them with a towel, rubbing the cool mountain water out of his unruly hair.

Standing at the front of the bus, the Preacher held forth. "I don't wanna see no more desertions," he said, hands in his back pockets as though he was arguing balls and strikes with a cross-eyed umpire. "We got a full slate of games ahead of us, all the way from here to Saskatchewan."

"How we gonna play with just eight players?" the Child Prodigy asked from a seat up front. "Is that even legal?"

"I don't rightly know what's legal and what ain't," the Preacher answered back. "Truth be known, I never expected anybody to walk off the team until their contract was up."

Fast Eddie was filing his fingernails in the seat behind Spitz. "Hell," he said, "these South Dakota bumpkins won't know the difference between what's legal and what ain't."

The Preacher considered this for a moment, rubbing his left hand over his stubbly jaw. "Do you think we can win with just eight?"

"I think we can win with just five," Eddie said, glancing up all cocky and piss-eyed as he sprayed fingernail filings around the place. "It's only in Omaha where they make you take an extra out every nine at bats."

Yanking a tattered card from the breast pocket of his dirty white shirt, the Preacher studied his lineup for a good long while. "We could go with two outfielders," he said at last, "Ray in left and the Prodigy in right. Spitzy, yer gonna have to play deep at short. With any luck, they won't touch Rube too hard tonight. How you feelin, Rube?"

Rube spat a wad of tobacco at the open bus window beside him and missed. Tobacco juice streaked the glass like sludge.

Betty said, "Ugh."

"Crisp," Rube said. "I'm feelin crisp like a three-day-old tortilla. They ain't gonna touch me tonight."

"Just don't pay no heed to the crowd," the Preacher warned him.

"They can blow zippidy-doo-dah out their arseholes fer all I care," Rube replied. "I won't give 'em the time of day."

"That's good then," the Preacher said. "We got to git a move-on. Did anybody fix that radiator hose this morning?"

"I wrapped some electrical tape around it," Clarence said. "That oughta hold til we git to Johnsonville."

"Good enough," the Preacher said. He sat down in the driver's seat and fired up the old beast. It clanked and sputtered and came to life with a throaty howl. The Preacher threw it into first gear, and the machine growled back at him belligerently. He fed it some gas, and they were on their way.

The sky darkened as they rode north out of the sacred hills. Ray nudged Spitz, who was sleeping next to him, in the ribs. "Looks like they ain't gonna be no ball game tonight," he said. There was a childish sense of deflation in Ray's voice that yanked at Spitz's heartstrings.

"Never can tell," Spitz said, "never can tell."

Dust lay everywhere along the side of the road. It drifted into ditches like snow. It covered ploughs in farmers' fields. Spitz saw a tarpaper shack all but hidden in a bank of dust.

It wasn't long before the dust seeped through the cracks in the closed bus windows. Soon there was a thin film of light brown dust on the seats and on the floor. Spitz could see a build-up of dust on Rube's broad shoulders. Betty found a white lace handkerchief in her handbag and pressed it firmly over her mouth and nose. Others coughed the dust out of their lungs.

They rode into Johnsonville that way, dust trailing them like the ghost of yesterday's regrets. It was a village like every other prairie village, the two-story houses brown and dirty-looking, paint peeling unhappily. Leafless cotoneaster hedges skirted the householders' lots like threadbare sentinels. The main street was devoid of people, but the buildings stood like an affirmation that humanity would one day prevail. One false front advertised the Johnson Pharmacy. Next to it was the Johnson and Johnson General Store, and across the street was the Johnson Brothers' Hardware. "Lotta Johnsons livin here," the Preacher announced.

He steered the bus into the Johnson and Son Garage, threw open the door and jumped down on to the pump island. A dirty looking kid straggled out of the building. "Yer Mister Johnson, I presume," the Preacher said.

"No," the kid snapped, "that's my dad yer talkin about." The kid's father came out of the building, as well, curious to see why a busload of strangers would be coming into town.

"Fill 'er up," the Preacher said. "And we could use some water fer the rad."

"Good luck with that," the kid's father drawled. "Town well went dry three weeks ago."

"Three weeks ago," the Preacher said. "Whatcha bin drinkin since then?"

"Beer and pop mostly," the senior Johnson said. "Don't know what we'll do when that runs out."

The ballpark, if that's what you wanted to call it, was situated at the edge of the village behind a one-room schoolhouse. The backstop was made of rough-hewn poplar poles and chicken wire. There wasn't a blade of grass on the infield and only the odd clump of quack grass beyond that. "Seems like a bum deal," Fast Eddie complained as he got off the bus, "to come away from the major leagues and play on this."

The home team was already out on the field, shagging fly balls. Spitz and the Preacher sat down on the slivery two-by-twelve that passed for a bench and watched. "Tall motherfuckers," the Preacher muttered.

"The bigger they are," said Spitz, "the harder we fall."

A big fellow, squeezed into a pair of coveralls that looked like a second skin, approached them from the other side of the diamond. He handed the Preacher a crumpled sheet of notepad paper. From the look of it, he'd been carrying that sheet of paper in his back pocket since Christ was a cowboy. The big fellow's face was grimy.

The Preacher perused the opposing team's lineup. "Lotta Johnsons playin tonight," he said.

"A few Swensons too," the big fellow replied.

"Yeah. So twenty-five bucks is our appearance fee."

"Meant to talk to you about that," the big fellow said. "Would you take twenty-five birds instead?"

"Twenty-five birds?"

"Chickens," the big fellow added. "They're good eatin."

"We'd prefer cash," the Preacher said.

"Ain't got no cash, but we can give you chickens."

The Preacher looked at him, steely-eyed. "Where do you got these fuckin chickens?"

"Johnson is bringin 'em to the game," the big fellow said. "He'll just load them on the bus while we're playing."

It turned out the Scandinavians could really play ball. They had a long streak of misery by the name of Johnson on the mound—

he was rumored to be a shirt-tail relation of the Big Train Walter Johnson himself—and the kid could throw heat. Maybe it was heartbreak at losing their cleanup man or maybe it was the ill effects of all that dust, but the Appalachian All-Stars did not fare well against the gawky kid. Spitz was 0 for 4 going into the sixth inning. The Preacher, who'd moved himself into the cleanup spot, had managed a measly single. Clarence had walked once, and then he'd stolen second and third without a slide. Betty had bunted him in, and the score was 1-1.

On the mound for the Appalachians, Rube had given up one run early. Spitz could see him talking to himself between pitches, and after that he settled down. In the bottom of the sixth, Rube struck out the side and performed front and back flips all the way off the field to the bench. "Jeez Louise," he exhorted his teammates, "you got to give me some support."

Spitz looked to the west. The sky had darkened to a dull brown, and low-lying clouds of something were stalking the landscape in plodding dinosaur steps. Everything went spooky and quiet while the Johnson kid threw his warmup pitches.

The Preacher batted first, flying out to centerfield. Spitz took a few practice swings and stepped up to the plate. He heard a mighty whoosh behind him, and then the dust storm blew in at ninety miles per hour. Spitz could barely see the pitcher, sixty feet away, and the late inning ball was a dirty brown that blended in nicely with the doom-laden cloud of vaporous dust. The first pitch went by him like a hanky out of a magician's hand. Spitz didn't see the ball, but he heard it smack into the catcher's mitt behind him. "Strike!" the umpire said.

Between gusts of wind, Spitz could see hoodoos of dust in the outfield, trembling giants of dust that seemed to be coming to the aid of the hometown team. He saw the second pitch well enough, right out of the pitcher's hand, but it was clearly a foot off the outside of the plate. The umpire called it a strike. "You got supper burnin on the stove?" Spitz asked. "Or is there something else you got to get home early for?"

The wind died down just as the pitcher released his third offering. Spitz could see that the pitch was also outside, but he refused to let the umpire control his fate. Stepping across the plate, he delivered a powerful wallop with his bat. The contact felt wholesome and good, and Spitz could tell from the solid crack that he'd hit the ball well. He stood at the plate and watched the orb climb, reaching for the other side of the snow fence that contained the field. He stood and watched as the wind surged and the mighty hoodoos of dust swirled in the outfield. He could have sworn that one of those hoodoos had a face and that it was the face of the devil. The ball kept climbing, against the wind now but climbing, and the hoodoo rose to meet it. At the last moment, the baseball disappeared into the agitated paws of the whirlwind. Spitz never saw where it landed. The wind rose up. Unanchored bases went skittering across the diamond like pillows in a pillow fight. Spitz hid his face behind his elbow to avoid the sandblasting that ensued.

"I'm callin this game," the umpire growled, "on account of the apocalypse."

The few fans that had been in attendance were hustling back to the village. Mothers scolded their children to hurry. "It's the end of the world," Spitz heard one woman say. "Best we put our affairs in order." The home team gathered their equipment from the bench and disappeared into a whirligig of flying debris.

"Everybody on the bus!" the Preacher shouted, but the bus, parked just behind the diamond, was nowhere in sight.

Most of the team had left the bench by the time Spitz got there. Ray was still sitting, his baseball glove over his eyes, squinting at the storm through the leather webbing. Spitz took him by the throwing hand. "C'mon buddy, we gotta get on the bus now."

"Ain't we gonna finish the game?"

"Game's been called," Spitz hollered into the wind. He pulled Ray vaguely along the chicken wire backstop in the direction where he thought the bus might be. They were lost in a hurricane of dust. Stumbling as the sand blasted them, pierced their skin like driving hail, they found their way to the backstop a second time.

"I'm ascared, Spitzy," Ray howled. "My head hurts."

"Just hang on to me," Spitz hollered back. "I won't let nothin bad happen to ya." With the maelstrom roaring around him, Spitz stopped and thought for a moment. He remembered that the bus was parked at a right angle on the visitor's side of the backstop, maybe thirty feet away. One hand on Ray and the other grazing the chicken wire, he traced the route to where the backstop ended. As the storm raged on, he executed an about turn and, shielding his face against the blast, edged his way toward where the bus might be. Banging his kneecap on the front fender, Spitz felt relief instead of pain. He edged his way to the door, and the door popped open, seemingly of its own accord.

"Glad you could make it!" the Preacher shouted from the driver's seat. "Get in before this wind blows us all away."

Spitz pushed Ray up the steps and climbed behind him into the vehicle. The air was thick with brown dust. As he edged toward the back of the bus, Spitz could see a host of chickens perched on the seats, eyes closed and wheezing.

"Wouldn't go back there if I were you," Betty said. "There's chicken doo everywhere."

"Got to get my stuff," Spitz muttered. He deposited Ray in the seat behind Betty and proceeded to the back of the bus. He felt the soft squish of chicken shit under his cleats and almost lost his footing. The chickens were fast asleep against the horror of the storm, but Spitz could hear their deep-throated purring. He found his habitual seat, found his woolen army blanket and brushed a wad of chicken manure off it. Picking up his green canvas duffle bag, he headed back to the seat beside Ray.

"So," the Preacher shouted, "are we all present and accounted for?"

"I think so," said the Prodigy.

Fast Eddie stood up and looked around. "Wait a minute," he said, low and unhappy. "Where's Rube?"

"Rube?" the Preacher replied. "I thought he was here."

"Should we send a posse out to look for him?" the Prodigy asked.

"That'd be certain death!" the Preacher shouted. "He's likely safe and sound in that schoolhouse out back."

"What if he ain't?" Eddie asked.

"You know as well as I do what Rube's like," the Preacher said. "A goddamn cat. He's got more lives than a goddamn cat."

A catalogue of Rube's misadventures was enumerated, more to calm the inhabitants of the bus than to enjoy them in their own right. There were the two ex-wives, one of whom had tried to run over him with a Studebaker coupe. The other had resorted to poison, but Rube had managed to digest the arsenic-laced tea with a minimum of discomfort. There was the time he'd doused himself with water and run into a burning house to rescue a puppy on the third floor. He'd singed most of the hair off his head with that escapade. And then there was the time, at the circus, when he volunteered to be shot out of a cannon. He'd missed the pool of water altogether, landing instead on the roof of a nearby house before straggling to his feet and exclaiming that he was indeed a human cannonball.

Thus assured, the All-Stars stopped their worrying or, at least, they hid their worries as they did their aches and pains. The chickens chucked and snored at the back of the bus. "Tell me again," Fast Eddie said. "Whose idea was it to accept these hens in lieu of payment?"

"Quit yer gripin," said the Preacher. "These chickens'll be good eatin along the way."

The windstorm howled against the rivets of the bus. It screeched like bent metal through the cracks in the windows. It rocked the hulking beast from wheel to wheel in an effort to topple it on its side. Betty pulled a blanket over her head to shut out the storm. Soon the others followed suit.

Spitz pulled his own blanket up over Ray, hung it like a tent between his own seat back and the seat back in front of him. "We'll be cozy in here," he whispered. Ray smiled and closed his eyes. Dust dry in his esophagus, Spitz thought about erosion. He thought about the pyramids in Egypt and the mausoleums in India. He thought about how nature breaks everything down, how all man's toil and sweat will come to nothing in the end. He thought about those things as the dust caked around him like the walls of his own grave.

6. Revival Meeting

No one could say when the storm abated.

Spitz had been dreaming death all night, dust clogging his nostrils. In his dream, he'd been lying on his back in a deep hole, and a spray of gravel was hitting his face. He'd heard them pronouncing his eulogy. "In the name of the Father," he'd heard them say, "and the Son…."

He was awakened by the Preacher, who was sitting crumpled and dirty at the front of the bus, bent over, hunched, and mumbling the Lord's Prayer to himself. "Our Father Who art in Heaven," Spitz thought he heard the Preacher say, "Hollywood be Thy name." He couldn't have heard the Preacher right.

Ray was still sleeping, curled up like a cat in his half of the bench seat. He stirred a little bit as Spitz tucked the army blanket around him. Spitz looked over his shoulder toward the back of the bus. The chickens that had been snoring throatily the night before were huddled and silent. Spitz maneuvered past Ray and tiptoed to the door. His teammates were mostly still asleep. The Prodigy was reading a thick book called *The Collected Works of William Shakespeare*. He was always reading when he wasn't playing baseball. "Goin to look fer Rube," Spitz whispered when he was at the Preacher's side.

"I'll tag along," the Preacher whispered back.

The door of the bus yawned open like the mouth of a thousand-year-old ogre, and the two men ventured out into the moonscape. There was a bank of dust six feet high that covered the first three planks of the wooden grandstand. There was a drift of soil behind the pitcher's mound that stretched all the way to where second base had been. The home run fence had blown down in the wind. Spitz and the Preacher surveyed the damage on the bus. The blue paint had been sandblasted to a dull grey. The lettering on the side of the bus was faded to the point where it was almost indecipherable.

"Christ," the Preacher muttered, "we suffered the wrath of God here last night."

Spitz wondered whether the dust storm could be blamed on God or on some other more malevolent power. "Let's go find Rube," he said.

The door of the schoolhouse was barricaded with sand. Spitz and the Preacher kicked at the sand, clawed it out of the way with their hands. Finally, the door was open, and the two men were standing inside on the cracked hardwood floor of the one-room school. They had expected to see Rube curled up in a corner or perhaps on the teacher's desk, happily asleep. He wasn't there.

They searched the outhouses and looked under the bus. They walked into town. The place looked deserted. Signs were blown down or uprooted. Shingles were missing from rooftops. There was no further evidence of human activity.

The Preacher pounded on the door of the fuel station for a good ten minutes. The old fellow who owned the place could, at last, be seen, through the plate glass window that fronted the station, straggling from the living quarters in the back. He was unshaven, with only a pair of tweed trousers hiked up by one suspender loop over his long johns. He unlocked the door. "I told ya, we ain't got no water."

"We're lookin fer one of our guys," the Preacher told him. "Big feller. Kinda quirky. He'd still be wearin his baseball uniform."

The elder Johnson scratched his stubbly chin. "Saw one of yer men walkin down the road outta town last night," he said. "Funniest goddamn thing I ever saw. Wind howlin around him. He just walked down the road and disappeared in a cloud of dust."

The Preacher looked at him, suspicious. "You sure he was one of ours'?"

"He was wearin a baseball uniform," the man said. "And it weren't a Johnsonville uniform. That much I know."

Spitz and the Preacher weren't willing to take the man's word for it. Only after they'd knocked on every door, searched every shed and back alley, were they convinced that Rube had done what he always did, which was to disappear at the slightest provocation.

Their teammates were awake and busy by thc time Spitz and the Preacher returned. They'd set about cleaning the inside of the bus. Clarence was scraping chicken doo off the seats with a small trowel that was normally used to scrape mud off his cleats. He'd set out a bowl of slough water for the chickens to drink and also a bowl of cracked oats from the large porridge sack that the Preacher had brought along. Betty, Ray, and the Prodigy were busy shaking dust off their blankets out behind the bus. Fast Eddie sat in his seat and filed his fingernails. He was above the mundane task of cleaning up.

"Well, we'd better skedaddle," the Preacher announced.

"What about Rube?" the Prodigy asked.

The Preacher threw open the bus door. "He's off on one of his walkabouts."

"How do you know?"

"We searched the village with a fine-toothed comb," the Preacher replied. "And a guy said he saw Rube heading down the road. Maybe we'll overtake him on the way into Bismarck."

The bus started with a wheeze and a cough, and they departed the village. Out in the countryside, they drove by pastures where the cattle lay dead, suffocated by the laden air they'd breathed. Stopping at a pond that was almost dry, they scooped up rangy green water in jugs and cups, pouring it into the hissing radiator and saving some of the precious liquid for the next time the brittle hose might burst. The chickens chuck chucked happily as they careened into North Dakota, and the humans on the bus momentarily forgot their woes. They headed north at a slow and steady pace, but they never saw Rube at the edge of the highway.

Bismarck was a tidy city, houses freshly painted, lawns watered and somehow not yet brown. It looked as though the dust storm had left the place unravaged. The streets were empty and clean. Children were not playing in front yards. There was no commerce of any kind, no tires changed in front of fuel stations, no farmers' markets, no baker selling dozens. You could have thrown a hand grenade down Main Street without hurting anyone. Spitz put it down to a strict observance of the Sabbath. Who knew these German Lutherans were so steadfast?

The Preacher steered through deserted streets, looking for the ballpark. He drove past the Governor's mansion on Avenue B. "Jesus Christ," he muttered, "what's goin on here?" The rest of the team, and some of the chickens, were glued to the windows of the bus, peering at a multitude of national guardsmen, armed and ready, at the circumference of the property. There was no sign of activity inside the mansion. The Preacher drove on.

They found the ballpark at the intersection of Washington Street and Front Avenue. It was the best diamond they'd seen in a long while. The infield was lush and green, watered from the Heart and Missouri Rivers. There was seating for a thousand people. The home run fence was purpose-built and eight feet high.

Two men were standing near the pitcher's mound, waiting. One of them was a chubby middle-aged white fellow in shirt sleeves. The other was a tall Black man in a crisp suit. Spitz and the Preacher walked out on to the field. The tall Black man pointed a bony finger at Spitz and smiled. "Spitzy," he drawled, "I was hopin I'd git to see you."

"The people you see when you ain't got a gun," Spitz replied. "What are you doin here, Satch?"

Satchel Paige grinned toothily at Spitz. "Well, you know, these boys hired me to pitch."

"I thought you was playin for the Crawfords."

Paige shrugged his shoulders and looked up at the clear, blue sky. "Had to go where the money was," he said, "and wherever baseball was bein played."

"Ain't gonna be no baseball played here today," the white fellow interrupted.

"Oh?" the Preacher said. "Why's that?"

"Governor declared martial law just this mornin," the chubby white guy replied. "You didn't see them troops outside his mansion?"

"Yeah, we saw 'em. What's goin' on?"

"The Feds are sayin he embezzled some of the taxpayers' hard-earned dollars. They're threatenin to cart the Governor off to jail."

"So he's holed up in that mansion of his?"

"Yup." The chubby fellow mopped sweat from his brow with a monogrammed handkerchief. "And he says he's gonna secede from the union."

"My oh my," said the Preacher.

"People are afraid to leave their houses."

The Preacher squinted at him in the afternoon sun. "You promised us a twenty-five-dollar appearance fee."

Kicking at the grass, the shirt-sleeved fellow said he was sorry, but he couldn't be held responsible for governors who embezzled money from the state coffers.

Paige shook his head unhappily. "It's jus' too bad," he said to Spitz. "I was lookin forward to handin you an ass-kickin."

The Preacher ignored Paige's comment. "How far is Mandan from here?"

"Bout six miles," the white guy said. "Why? What's in Mandan?"

"Dunno," said the Preacher. "Guess we'll find out."

Paige punched Spitz playfully in the shoulder. "Say, is Clarence Harms on that bus with you?"

"He is."

"Tell him he still owes me ten bucks."

As they were walking back to the bus, the Preacher spat a wad of tobacco on the ground. "Fuckin Paige thinks he's the best pitcher in all of baseball."

"He is," Spitz replied.

"Better than you?" the Preacher asked.

"Better than anyone I ever seen."

Twenty minutes later, the Preacher parked the bus outside a tall white church in Mandan. "Spitz, you come with me," he said before stepping off the vehicle. They walked to the manse behind the church.

A bespectacled man in his thirties, with a sensitive face and a thin-boned build, met them at the front door. He was wearing a thread-bare suit, probably the same suit he'd worn at the service earlier. "You the local minister?" the Preacher asked.

"Yes, I am."

"What's attendance bin like in yer church?"

"Hasn't been great," the minister told him. "These are trying times, and in trying times people sometimes fall away from the fold."

The Preacher smiled beneficently. "I believe we can be of some help if that's the case."

"But tell me," the local minister said, "what is your name?"

"Forgive my lack of grace," the Preacher replied. He reached into his shirt pocket and pulled out a business card. "I'm Preacher Allan Bentham, formerly of the Philadelphia Athletics and the Durham Bulls. Me and my team of baseball all-stars are currently traversing this fair land. We play baseball when we can, and we offer revival meetings on other days."

The minister's mouth was agape. "Preacher Bentham?" he said. "I used to follow the baseball reports quite closely in the newspaper. When I could afford the newspaper."

The Preacher smiled sidelong at Spitz. "And allow me to introduce Spitball McKague."

"Spitball McKague!" The local minister was almost too flustered to shake Spitz's hand, but then he said, "Well, sir, I am pleased to meet you."

"Pleased to meet you too, Reverend," Spitz replied. It was a full minute before the minister remembered to let go of Spitz's hand.

"You a baseball fan?" the Preacher asked.

"Baseball is the game that God created when we threw off the British yoke."

"Well, you'll have to forgive me," the Preacher said. "The Athletics never got outta last place the whole time I played for them."

A shy smile flashed across the minister's face. "I was a Yankee fan back then anyway."

The Preacher barked out a laugh. "Looks like that's something I'll have to forgive you for." He rested his gnarled hand on the minister's shoulder and spoke to him in hushed tones. "Do you think the locals might show up at the church tonight," he asked, "if word got out that Allan Bentham was preachin at a revival meetin?"

"I believe they would."

"And do you think that such a revival meetin might help to bring them back into the fold?"

"It can't hurt."

"And if I took up a collection," the Preacher said, "would it be all right if I offered your church a tithe of, say, twenty per cent?"

"That would be more than fair."

A smile creased the Preacher's weathered face. "Come back to the bus with me," he said. "I wanna introduce you to Fast Eddie Kramer."

The church was packed to the rafters that night. Sitting in a tall chair near the pulpit, the Preacher cultivated a pleasant and holy demeanor. He had resurrected his vestments from a duffle bag behind the driver's seat of the bus and, although it was wrinkled and unwashed, the garment still lent him an ethereal air. The congregants, many of whom had not been to church in some time, hummed with excitement. It was as if "It Happened One Night" had finally come to the town's movie theatre, and the locals were at last able to see what the excitement was about. Spitz and Clarence stood near the doors of the church, shaking hands with the congregants as they entered and sometimes signing autographs. Both men were decked out in the suits they'd been told to bring along on the tour. Fast Eddie and Ray waited off to the side of the nave, wooden collection plates in their hands. Betty and the Prodigy were in the minister's office at the back of the church, preparing the bread and wine that had been provided by the local minister for communion.

It was after eight in the evening by the time the parishioners were seated. The local minister rose and proceeded to the steps in front of the altar. "It is good to see such a massive turnout," he announced, not without a note of irony. "I'm sure none of you have come here this evening just because Preacher

Bentham is offering communion or because Spitball McKague and Fast Eddie Kramer are here as celebrants." The congregants broke into spontaneous laughter and then applause. "And I'm equally sure that all of you will be back here next Sunday," the minister said, more serious now, "when we celebrate the nativity of Saint John the Baptist." Remaining silent at that suggestion, the parishioners looked shiftily about. "So without further ado," the minister continued, sounding halfway between a stadium announcer and an auctioneer at a cattle sale, "let me introduce the former big league catcher and ordained minister—the Very Reverend Alan Bentham!"

Climbing reverentially to the pulpit, the Preacher looked out at the assembly and gathered his thoughts. For a moment Spitz wondered if he had forgotten his routine, but the Preacher was pausing for effect. After a moment, he cleared his throat and announced, in a voice reminiscent of those old-time umpires who worked before Bill Klem invented hand signals, "Gossip! Idle talk and rumor! Progenitor of hate and greed and envy! Ladies and gentlemen, I am here this evening to speak about the evils of gossip. We all know that gossip is a sin, and yet we all indulge ourselves in that sin!"

Spitz glanced over at Fast Eddie as the word *gossip* was repeated. Eddie looked smaller than his usual rangy self and decidedly more uncomfortable. His eyes bore into the empty collection plate in front of him, like he was looking for the meaning of life in the grain of the wood. Spitz began to wonder if he'd really done what he was accused of.

The Preacher struck an orator's pose, one hand on the edge of the pulpit, the other directed at the congregation. "Gossip is a sign that we are not active in our faith," he continued. "If we have time to gossip, we are not as busy as Christians ought to be. And yet we do gossip. As the Proverbs remind us, 'The words of a gossip are like choice morsels; they go down to a man's inmost parts.'" The Preacher paused again, appraising his audience as a shepherd appraises sheep. "Brothers and sisters, I'm sure you've all heard of the plight of Joe Jackson, former left fielder for the Chicago White Sox. Shoeless Joe, as he was called, was a sharecropper's son from South Carolina. He could neither read nor write. And yet he was accused of the most heinous crime a baseball player can commit. He was accused, brothers and sisters, of throwing the World Series of 1919." Well acquainted with this accusation, the parishioners nudged one another and whispered among themselves. The Preacher found another level for his diatribe and lowered his voice a full octave. "I knew Shoeless Joe Jackson, ladies and gentlemen, and I was proud to call him my friend. And I can promise you that Shoeless Joe Jackson was no more capable of throwing a ball game than I am of flying to the moon. But gossip, brothers and sisters, gossip brought him low."

The Preacher went on like this, without a note or a piece of paper in his hand, for the better part of an hour. He referred to James 5:9 ("Do not grumble against each other, brothers, or you will be judged") and to Proverbs 13:3 ("He who guards his lips guards his life, but he who speaks rashly will come to ruin"). He prayed. The organ fired up, and the Preacher led the congregation as they sang "I Love to Tell the Story." Betty and the Prodigy took their places in front of the altar, doling out bread and wine. After the communion, Eddie and Ray passed around the collection plate. The offering was not good, but it was better than expected. There was much shaking of hands at the back of the church, when the meeting was over, and incessant gabbing about baseball heroics in years gone by.

When all was said and done, the Preacher joined his crew on the bus in the church parking lot. As night had fallen again, the chickens roosted silently at the back of the vehicle. The Preacher produced a bottle of communion wine that had been surreptitiously lifted from a cupboard in the minister's office. Uncorking the bottle, he passed it around to whomever would take a swig. "God helps them that helps themselves," he announced. "Stick with me, and I'll have you fartin through silk in no time."

7. True North

They headed north that night, following the Missouri River almost as far as Washburn. Stopping in an abandoned farmyard along the way, the All-Stars tore sticks of lumber off an ancient, disused barn and made a fire. There was no water in the well. Spitz tried to prime the pump with a bit of slough water they'd saved, but it was no use. He reefed on the pump handle for a good half hour. The inner mechanism of the pump sounded gravelly and full of rust. No water was produced.

In the meantime, Ray and Betty trekked a mile overland to the river and returned with pails full of the gleaming liquid, their arms a foot longer for the travail. The rest of the team took turns dipping tin cups into one of the pails and drinking until their mighty thirsts were slaked. Spitz could not remember a time when cool, clear water tasted so good.

Clarence knew a thing or two about killing chickens. He snatched four of the sleeping fowl from their roosts at the back of the bus. They squawked and gurgled out of their deep standing-up sleep as Clarence hauled them away. The other chickens, roosting still, opened one eye to witness the abduction of their mates and then chose to forget the entire matter. Out behind the bus, Clarence slit the throats of the four sacrificial hens and released their headless bodies, then watched them skitter across the abandoned farmyard. The frenzy of murder ended only when the chickens had finally bled out, lying like feathery mounds in the moonlight.

One of the pails, full of water, was steaming over the fire. Gathering up the dead chickens, Clarence dipped each of them in boiling water and began ripping sticky feathers from the fat carcasses. Cutting a deft incision around the bowels of each bird, he ripped intestines out and tossed them into the fire. Then, skewering each fowl on a sharpened aspen sapling, he turned the birds slowly over the fire until the smell of death was off them, until they smelled like something resembling fried chicken.

When they were roasted, the birds were a tasty treat. The players sat around the fire, some on wooden chairs rescued from the old farmhouse, enjoying wings and drumsticks and speaking of the day's adventures. After the fire had died down, they climbed back on the bus to enjoy a good night's sleep, snuggled in old army blankets or under long coats.

Spitz woke in the darkness. He'd heard movement outside the bus. Glancing over his shoulder, he thought he saw a light inside the abandoned farmhouse. Was it a light, or was it the glint of the full moon off the window glass? He couldn't be sure. The surviving chickens grumbled at the back of the bus as Spitz slid out of his seat. Sentenced to a deep slumber by the evening's exertions, the Preacher did not even open an eye when Spitz jostled through the half-open door.

Once outside in the moonlight, Spitz could clearly see a coal-oil lamp flickering in the window of the farmhouse. He proceeded across the yard and through the open door of the wood frame house. As he entered, he saw an old man seated at the scratched wooden table. The chairs, which had been stationed around the fire earlier in the evening, were back in their proper place.

The old man turned his head to look at Spitz. It was the same man he had seen at the construction site in Des Moines. He was decked out in a crumpled white suit with a fedora to match, but his face was white and stony as alabaster. His white hair had grown to an unmanageable length. "I've been waiting for you," the old man said.

Frozen before him, Spitz waited for the revolver to appear. "Who are you?"

"Farewell, thou child of my right hand," the old man said, "and joy."

Spitz was not easily moved to fear, but he found himself trembling. "What do you want with me?"

The old man pushed back his chair and stood up. "My sin was too much hope of thee, loved boy." Spitz could see that the man was still shoeless, but he was also spryer than a man of his age should be. He glided past Spitz and out the open door.

"Where are you going?" Spitz asked.

"True north."

Spitz followed him out into the yard, past the bus where his teammates roosted with the chickens, and out into a barren field. The old man walked ahead of him at a regular pace, but Spitz found it difficult to keep up. He led Spitz to the banks of the river. Fed by the cool, clear stream, the grasses on the riverbank had grown to a stupendous height. Spitz could see yarrow in the moonlight. He could smell its heavy scent. The cattails stood along the path, dispensing pollen in the night air. The pollen settled like snowflakes on Spitz's shoulders and then thickened into a blizzard. Spitz could no longer see the old man in front of him. Pollen was in his eyes like death. It clogged his nasal cavities and filled his mouth and dammed up his ears. Fatigued by the journey and having lost sight of his guide, Spitz lay down in the tall grass by the side of the river and slept.

It was broad daylight when Spitz woke up. He heard the throaty gurgle of the river and felt the morning dew on his clothes. Sitting up amongst the grasses and the cattails, he looked around. His guide was nowhere to be seen. Spitz had left his pocket watch back on the bus. Judging by the sun, he thought it might be ten o'clock. Spitz could tell where east was, and he scrambled up the steep bank in the direction of the abandoned farmyard. Fearing that the bus might have left without him, Spitz quickened his pace.

He was relieved when he could see the farmyard again and the bus, a tattered grey, still sitting there. As he got closer, Spitz could see activity out in the yard. The fire was smoldering again, and his teammates were cleaning up after the morning meal. The hood of the bus stood open, and the Preacher was balanced on the bumper, wrapping tape around the radiator hose.

Ray was the first to get sight of Spitz as he walked briskly into the yard. "Where you bin, Spitzy?" he asked.

"Just out for a walk."

"I was worried about you."

"No need to worry ever, Ray. I can take care of myself."

"Still, you had me worried."

Betty threw dishwater on the fire, smoke and ash rising from the cinders. Spitz and Ray hauled the clean dishes back up to the bus. Having completed his repairs, the Preacher slammed the hood shut. "Minot, here we come!" he shouted. "Let's roll."

The road to Minot was unexciting. Treeless prairie replaced hills and forests as the bus jostled north along the gravel. The chickens grumbled and chucked.

It didn't help that Spitz had missed breakfast. His empty stomach rose and fell with every pothole in the gravel road. He was nauseous, but his belly had nothing in it except air.

As they neared Minot, Spitz noticed a man walking on the side of the road a few hundred yards ahead of the bus. Hearing the rattling engine behind him, the man turned and stuck out his thumb. He looked to be wearing a tattered baseball uniform. His hair was grey with dust, and his baseball cap was gone. His face was smudged and streaked with blood. Large as life and twice as ugly, Rube smiled toothily as the bus approached. The Preacher braked, and the bus squealed to a stop. Rube climbed aboard.

"What the hell happened to you?" the Preacher asked him.

Rube grinned. "Got myself involved with a buncha hobos. One of 'em tried to steal my chaw."

"Well, take a seat," the Preacher said. "We gotta be in Minot within the hour."

Rube walked down the aisle towards a seat. "What's with all these chooks?"

"They came in lieu of an appearance fee," the Prodigy told him.

"Shitty birds," Rube said. "Never did like 'em much, back on the farm." He found a seat beside Betty. "Hey, good-lookin," he said, putting his arm around her. "Long time, no see."

Betty had been filing her fingernails whenever the bumpy road allowed her to do so. She held the pointed file under Rube's chin like a knife. "Keep your hands to yourself," she said.

Minot was a clean city. Hotels and restaurants and taverns lined the clean streets. Businessmen looked dapper in their crisp suits, and ladies in their broad hats and finery roamed the fashionable clothing stores. Small as it was, the city reminded Spitz of a little Chicago. Prohibition had left its mark but only in a good way. There were new schools and universities, churches and cemeteries. People drove new cars and trucks.

The local baseball team was fashionable, as well, decked out in spotless white uniforms and jaunty hats. They played a brand of baseball that was also jaunty and fashionable. The game was called on account of darkness after seven innings, with the All-Stars winning by a score of twenty-seven to nothing.

After the handshake, Spitz noticed a tall woman with bobbed hair talking to Betty at the backstop. She was the kind of woman that used to wait in parking lots for Spitz when he played big league ball. She was decked out in high heels and a flapper dress, a little out of style by down east standards, but still pretty.

Rube was immediately interested. "Who's that talkin to Betty?" he asked Spitz when they were back on the bench.

"Dunno," Spitz said. "Must be an old friend."

"She sure is pretty."

A moment later, Betty came over to the bench, looking like a cat with a sparrow in its mouth. "What time are we leaving in the morning?" she asked the Preacher.

"Early."

"Well, I've found a friend," she said. "We're going to the moving picture."

"The moving picture?" the Preacher replied. "Starin at that flickerin screen ain't good for the eyesight."

"I'll be okay," Betty said. "See you back here at midnight."

She boarded the bus before any of her teammates were ready to do so and, when she came out again, Spitz could see that she was all dolled up in a yellow dress, makeup on her face. The flapper was there to receive her. They walked into the cool evening of the city, looking like long-lost sisters, walking arm in arm as women do.

Paid in full before they left the ballpark, the Preacher and his men found a restaurant at the edge of the city that could countenance white folks and African Americans seated together at a table. They ate Denver sandwiches, drank hot coffee and orange juice, and chattered about the game. Clarence was particularly enlivened. He'd gone five for five with a triple and two doubles. The scar-faced fellow that they'd seen twice along the way was, by coincidence, toying with a piece of lemon meringue pie at a far table. He sat there with a friend, a burly fellow who nursed a cup of coffee. They both seemed to take great interest in the baseball players and their conversation.

When the meal was finished and the team was making its way back to the bus, they encountered the scar-faced man in the parking lot. A broad-brimmed fedora was pulled low over his face. His demeanor was different than it had been when he'd stopped to help with the flat tire three days earlier. He was brusque and business-like, almost pugilistic. He stepped in front of Eddie as he was trying to board the vehicle. "Yer Fast Eddie Kramer," he said. His voice was raspy and low like a gun with a silencer. The burly man was standing right behind him.

"That's right," Eddie said, smirking. "You want my autograph?"

"It ain't yer autograph I'm after."

"Then what is it you're after?" Eddie asked, his voice turning hard and suspicious.

The scar-faced man glared up at him. "Ever heard of Al Capone, Eddie?"

"I've heard of him." Eddie wasn't smirking anymore.

"I'll bet you have," the man said. "Specially since you were on the payroll."

Eddie looked over his shoulder to see who was listening. The Preacher and the other guys had heard it all. "I wasn't on no payroll," Eddie hissed.

The scar-faced man was stocky but six inches shorter than Eddie. His angry lips twitched. "Al's in jail now," the man said, "but that don't mean his associates ain't out here, lookin after his interests."

The Preacher stepped in front of Eddie like a good catcher does after a hit batsman. "I thought you was a fan," he said to the scar-faced man.

"I got no gripe with you," the man said back, "but I ain't no fan of this guy."

"I think you better move on," the Preacher replied, "before you fall down and hurt yourself."

There was a moment of silence when all Spitz could hear was the sound of mosquitos buzzing and the clanking of a distant trainyard. The man regarded Eddie cooly. "Oh, I'll move on all right," he said. His words spewed like sulfur out of his mouth. "But this asshole better keep his head on a swivel." Without another word, the scar-faced man and his burly friend turned and walked back to their jet-black Ford.

Eddie stood there, shamefaced, as the rest of the team looked on. The Preacher rested his hand on Eddie's shoulder. "Who shat in his cornflakes this morning?" he said as they watched the Ford screech out of the parking lot and heard the furious rumble of its V-8 engine on the highway.

"Get me outta this town," Eddie said, quietly.

"Outta this town?" the Preacher replied. "Buddy, we're gonna get you right outta this country soon as Betty comes back from the movies."

They got back to the baseball diamond well before midnight, but Betty wasn't there. The parking lot was quiet and dark. Eddie's head was indeed on a swivel; he looked about furtively as though he expected Bonnie and Clyde to show up at any moment. Ray played "Big Bad Bill Is Sweet William Now" on his harmonica. The Preacher tapped his fingers on the steering wheel, keeping time. One o'clock rolled around, and Betty still hadn't arrived.

At one thirty, Spitz decided to take a walk. Throwing on his old Red Sox jacket, he stepped off the bus and headed toward the center of the city. The streets were empty and garish now, lit by incandescent bulbs and the odd neon sign. Desertion made the sidewalks seem capacious.

It wasn't long before he encountered a policeman, walking a beat, a mountain of a fellow with an Irish brogue. The policeman emerged from the entryway of a five-and-dime as Spitz was walking by. He was wearing a billed cap and a dark uniform with a belt crisscrossing from shoulder to hip. "What's a young git like you doin out on a night like this?" thc policeman asked. His tone was low and guttural.

Spitz sized up the officer. He figured he could outrun the guy, but the holster by the policeman's left pocket made him reevaluate that strategy. "Just out fer a stroll," Spitz replied.

The big policeman chuckled threateningly. "Nobody's out fer a stroll at one-tharty in the mornin."

"I'm lookin for my sister," Spitz said.

The officer squinted at him as the neon light above the storefront flickered on and off. His eyes were pig-like. "Yer sister? What the divil would yer sister be doin out at this hour?"

"She went to the moving picture," Spitz said. "I'm goin down to the theater to pick her up."

"The moving picture let out hours ago," the policeman replied, edging closer to Spitz. The palm of his hand was resting fidgety on his nightstick. "Yer not makin a whole lotta sense here, son."

Spitz decided that the best defense was a good offense. "Is it against the law to walk down the street in this city?"

The officer smiled wryly. "It is, now, if yer up to no good. It is, if yer one of them hobos lookin to burn the place down."

"I haven't done anything wrong."

"I'm gonna need to see a piece of identification," the policeman said. His fat fingers were now firmly around the handle of the nightstick. Spitz fished his wallet out of the pocket of his dungarees and showed the policeman his driver's license. "Thomas McKague from Georgia," the policeman said. Spitz was almost surprised that the man could read. "You, my son, are a long way from home." He proffered the license back to Spitz but, in the process of handing it to him, clamped a steel cuff on Spitz's right wrist. The other end of the cuff chain was attached to the officer's belt.

"What the hell?" Spitz said.

"You'll be comin with me down to the station, my fine fella," the policeman replied, "and we'll git to the bottom of who you really are."

8. Crossing the Line

The police station, like every other building in Minot, was tidy. It looked a bit like an office building where businessmen and accountants might work. As they walked through the double doors into the public area, Spitz was impressed by the spotlessness of the stone floor.

A fatigued sergeant was working the front desk. He looked up from his paperwork and gave Spitz a cursory glance. "Who's this now?"

"Can't be sure, Sergeant Flummerfelt," said the officer, still attached to Spitz by a handcuff chain. "He showed me a Georgia driver's license." The officer yanked on the chain, pulling Spitz closer to the desk.

"Let's take a gander at that license then," said the sergeant.

Spitz handed the officer his license, and the officer placed it on the desk. Sergeant Flummerfelt looked at it with cynical and tired eyes. He studied Spitz's face, then looked again at the faded photograph on the license. "Thomas McKague?" he said.

"Yeah," Spitz replied.

The sergeant's tone changed in an instant. "Spitball McKague? Lately of the Boston Red Sox?"

"That's me."

A skylight seemed to open in the ceiling of the station, with moonlight shining through. There was light in the sergeant's eyes, as well. "My cousin saw you play one time, back east. Said you had a spitball that dropped like a marble off a tabletop."

"I don't pitch anymore," Spitz replied.

"So I heard," said Flummerfelt. "Are you playin for that all-star team that rolled into town this afternoon?"

"I am."

The sergeant turned his attention to his officer, not in a kind way. "Have you never heard of Spitball McKague, Officer McIlroy?"

The officer looked shame-faced and side-long at Spitz. "I don't follow baseball," he said.

"Well, you should," Flummerfelt replied. "It's the greatest game in this great land." He smiled at Spitz again. "I must apologize for Officer McIlroy's actions here," he said. "We've had a lot of problems with vagrants of late."

"Tain't no thing," Spitz replied.

Flummerfelt looked expectantly at his officer for a long minute. "Well, don't just stand there, McIlroy. Release this man."

The big police officer fumbled in one pocket, and then another, for the key to the handcuffs. Spitz could see him trembling as he tried to insert the key in the lock. When the cuff was finally snapped open, Spitz massaged his wrist and flexed his fingers. "Terrible sorry," McIlroy said. "I had no idea."

"No hard feelings," Spitz replied, and then he turned to the sergeant. "I'm lookin for my sister," he said. "She's a ball player, just like me."

Flummerfelt blanched, looking like he didn't know whether to spit or steal third base. "Your sister?"

"Strawberry blonde," Spitz replied. "Last I saw of her, she was wearin a yellow dress."

There was an exchange of glances between Flummerfelt and McIlroy. "Your sister?" Flummerfelt said again.

"Yeah," Spitz replied. "She's about five foot five."

The sergeant cleared his throat. "We brought a lady in here earlier this evening," he admitted, "on a charge of public indecency."

It was Spitz's turn to be flummoxed. "Indecency?"

Flummerfelt looked at him with hang-dog eyes, almost ashamed to say what he had to say next. "She was committing a rash act with a flap in a movie theater."

"My sister?" Spitz said. "Are you sure?"

The sergeant perused the ledger on the desk in front of him. "We had no idea she was your sister," he explained. "She had no identification on her. Told us her name was Betty Anne Lindblom."

Spitz had to think fast. "That's her married name." He leaned over the sergeant's desk, confidentially. "I wouldn't want her husband to find out about this."

"There's no need to worry," Flummerfelt said, glancing sidelong at Officer McIlroy. "We can be very discreet here. Can't we, McIlroy?"

"Oh, yes sir," McIlroy said, "we can be tight-lipped as they come."

"She's never done anything like this before," Spitz said.

Flummerfelt placed a comforting hand on Spitz's shoulder. "I'm sure she hasn't."

"Can I have a word with her?" Spitz asked.

"Certainly, you may," Flummerfelt said. "She's in one of the holding cells downstairs."

The two police officers led Spitz through a door and down a hallway with a scrubbed green linoleum floor toward the holding cells. There were yellow lights on the walls every fifty feet. They descended a flight of stairs and arrived at the first cell. It was cold and dark.

Spitz could see the hunched body of a woman in a thin yellow dress, her back towards him. She was staring at the cinderblock wall, looking small and fox-like, shivering against the cold. A third police officer sat on a wooden chair behind Spitz, keeping a watchful eye on Betty. Spitz glared at the man. "What's this guy lookin at?"

"We keep a guard down here all night long," Flummerfelt explained, "in case of a disturbance."

"She's the only prisoner you got," Spitz said.

"The girl she was with ran off," Flummerfelt replied, "before she could be apprehended."

Spitz edged closer to the cell, grasping the bars in his hands. "You all right, Betty?"

Betty didn't respond.

Spitz looked at her for a long time, and then he turned to Flummerfelt. "I don't have any money," he said, "but I'd be willing to give you this Red Sox jacket if you could see your way to droppin the charges." The sergeant looked at his subordinates, all the while considering Spitz's offer. "It's the genuine article," Spitz added. "Same one Babe Ruth used to wear."

Flummerfelt inspected the jacket for a moment. "What size is that?"

"Extra large."

The sergeant looked at the ceiling and then at McIlroy and the other officer. "I think we can do that for an ex-major leaguer," he said at last. "Couldn't we, McIlroy? Maybe in the dark of that movie theater, you couldn't be too sure what you saw? Isn't that right?"

McIlroy protested. "I saw what I saw."

"Yes," Flummerfelt said, "but in the dark you couldn't be too sure."

"Well," McIlroy acquiesced, "I guess I couldn't be a hundred per cent sure."

"That's good sportsmanship now," said Flummerfelt. "I'm certain this can all be forgotten." He held out his hand. Spitz unburdened himself of the Red Sox jacket and handed it to the sergeant. Almost lasciviously, Flummerfelt ran his fingers over the melton wool. "Winterhalt," he said to the guard on the chair, "set this lady free."

Whether Betty heard any, or all, of this, she never let on. Her eyes fixed on the wall in front of her, she continued to shiver with her back to Spitz and the policemen. Winterhalt unlocked the cell and helped Betty to a standing position. He walked her over to Spitz, who took her by the arm. She did not look in Spitz's eyes. "C'mon sis," Spitz said, "let's get outta here."

They walked in silence through the empty streets toward the ballpark, the darkness pressing down hard against them. Betty kept her eyes trained on the spotless sidewalk through most of the journey. At last, when they were in sight of the park, she turned to Spitz and said, "Please don't tell the Preacher about this."

"The Preacher's a man of God," Spitz said. "If anybody's gonna understand, it would be him."

Betty stopped in her tracks, and Spitz stopped too. "No," she said, "he'll boot me off the team."

"I think you underestimate the man," Spitz replied.

There were tears in Betty's eyes, and then her body was wracked with paroxysms of grief. She collapsed into Spitz's arms, and he held her there, as moths fluttered around the streetlight over their heads. Spitz had not held a woman in his arms for many months. When Betty was finally able to speak, her voice quivered. "I'm sorry I had to get you involved."

Spitz looked at her and smiled. "We're on the same team."

Betty managed a smile too. "Looks like I owe you a jacket."

"I wouldn't worry about it," Spitz replied. "Never liked that jacket much anyway. All that history made my back itch."

He handed Betty a handkerchief, and she dried her eyes. "I hope you don't think I'm a bad person."

"I don't think that," Spitz said. "And I won't say a word to anyone, if it makes you feel better."

Betty said thank you, and she kissed him on the cheek. It was indeed like being kissed by one's sister, Spitz thought, kind of like playing hard and ending in a tie. They resumed their walk toward the ballpark and the bus, happy they had seemed to arrive at an understanding. But Spitz didn't understand such things. He'd heard that there were women like Betty, but he hadn't quite believed it. He resolved to wipe the entire incident from his mind as though it were a bad inning on the field. A short memory is best, he told himself, in love and baseball. He'd once heard Connie Mack say something to the same effect. As they walked toward the ballpark, Spitz got to thinking how hard love is to find and how you'd better latch on with all your might if you ever find it.

They headed north in the dark toward the border. Spitz had never been to Canada before. In his imagination, it was a vast plain of ice and snow, inhabited by mounted policemen wearing red serge jackets and snow-blind trappers traversing the vast wilderness by dogsled. There was a mystique about the untamed nature of the country.

The road out of Minot was surprisingly well maintained, probably owing to the continuous trafficking of hard liquor from above the forty-ninth parallel. There were few cars on the highway that late in the evening. Spitz was surprised when he lowered his window near the border at Portal and realized that the temperature had not dropped twenty degrees.

He was also surprised to learn that the border crossing was closed after midnight. The Preacher stopped the bus in front of the wood frame Customs building on the Canadian side. He got out and pounded on the door of the office. There was no response. No Mountie came out, fastening the gold buttons on his jacket. The Preacher got back on the bus and slammed it into gear. "Welcome to Canada, folks!" he shouted.

Betty spoke up. "Shouldn't we wait for the Customs office to open?"

"What are they gonna do to us?" the Preacher asked. "These Canucks are more concerned with rum runners headin south than with baseball teams goin north."

"We could get in a shitload of trouble," Spitz said, "crossin borders without permission."

"Canadians are a polite, gentle sort," the Preacher replied. "Long as we mind our p's and q's, there won't be no trouble."

The bus lurched forward and picked up speed along the gravel road. Soon they were out of sight of the border crossing. In the moonlight, Spitz could see that the landscape was not appreciably different than it had been two hours before in North Dakota. The crops were burnt and brown. The farmhouses were unpainted. Ancient cars, some of them converted to horse drawn wagons, stood at the ready in windblown yards. There were barns and there were cattle. Clotheslines, bereft of shirts and sheets, were strung between four-by-fours. There was comfort in that, comfort in learning that borders are not fixed and firm, that people are just people pretty much everywhere on this earth. They have the same wants and needs, the same longing for home and hearth, the same joy in the rise of the morning sun and in the evening twilight.

9. No Man's Land

They pulled into a town called Estevan just as the sun was coming up. A bituminous yellow fog was in the air, and the place smelled like used oil. The Preacher parked the bus near a railway siding. There was a rusty, burned-out trash barrel beside the tracks, probably left there by hobos who'd ridden the rails all the way from Chicago. Plenty of wasted coal lay along the siding, where steam locomotives would have stopped to replenish their supply. Spitz, Ray, and Betty gathered stray lumps and carried them to the trash barrel. Their hands and faces were grimy with coal dust by the time the sun had fully risen. A fire was soon lit, and the players warmed themselves in its glow. The Preacher found a metal grate, part of a disused sieve, which he placed over top of the barrel. He brewed a pot of coffee on the grate, covering his nose and mouth with a handkerchief and growing morose at the resemblance of this sky to the sky over the Argonne Forest. To the south, he could see high ridges of sand that reminded him of no-man's-land.

Salt pork was sizzling on the grate in a cast-iron frying pan as the town came awake. A flat-bed truck loaded with miners rumbled by. Then a Mountie pulled up in a Model A. He looked crisp and washed and blond in the early morning sun as he climbed out of the car and approached the Preacher. He spoke in an unmistakable British accent. "Good day, old sport," he said to the Preacher. "Are you tramps or are you miners?"

The Preacher lowered the handkerchief that was covering his nose. "Neither," he said, surly and unkind. "We're baseball players."

The Mountie smiled, flashing the dimples on his cheeks. "Baseball players?"

"Yes." The Preacher always had an edge, but he was edgier that day than Spitz had ever seen him.

"In town for a friendly match?"

"We are."

"That's jolly good then," the Mountie said.

This calmed the Preacher down a bit. "Can you point us in the direction of the baseball field?"

The Mountie pointed with a gloved hand. "Just up the road, old flower. You can't miss it."

The baseball diamond was a red sand affair with a quack grass outfield. There was a wooden grandstand, four tiers high, behind a chicken wire backstop. A two-by-twelve length of fir, balanced on ten-gallon pails, served as the visitors' bench. The base paths were deep troughs pounded into the ground by years of baserunning. There was no home run fence.

Because there was little else to do in the town, the All-Stars arrived at the diamond early. They tossed the ball leisurely on the outfield grass, gradually lengthening the distance until they were throwing long-toss from one foul line to the other. Curious townsfolk came to watch, parking their jalopies and buckboards and Bennett buggies along the perimeter of the field. Some of them made a picnic of it, spreading woolen blankets on the ground in front of their vehicles and munching sandwiches.

The coal mine didn't shut down until seven o'clock, so the game had to start late. Most of the hometown players were miners as Spitz could tell from their blackened faces and the circles of virgin white skin around their eyes. They trudged on to the field, backs bent, haggard from their brutal work. Some coughed blood into handkerchiefs or horked it on the barren soil.

The Preacher was behaving more and more erratically. Gathering the team together near the bench, he uttered something about Alvin York and storming the machine gun nests. He was visibly shaking as he insisted on holding hands for a pre-game prayer. His voice was faltering too. He pleaded with God for the safe passage of everyone on the team. The ceremony ended with a battle cry. "Did you think you were gonna live forever?" he said.

Straightening up considerably as the game went on, the local boys played with workmanlike resolve. A big straw-haired kid was pitching for them. He could throw hard but not straight, and lack of control was his main asset. None of the All-Stars were digging into the batter's box with him on the mound.

It got dark slowly on the plains. The sun seemed to settle on the western horizon and rest there for hours, turning a bright yellow and then a shade of orange and finally blood-red. The All-Stars were winning 10-1 by then, and Spitz was sure the game would be called on account of darkness. But it wasn't called. At the top of the fourth inning, the home team meandered out on to the field wearing hardhats with headlamps strapped to the front of them. They seemed expert at directing the glaring beams of those headlamps into the eyes of the All-Star batters. With nine miner's lamps focused bright upon him, Spitz lost the ball altogether in his next at-bat. The umpire called, "Strike!"

"Strike?" Spitz asked. "Did he even throw the pitch yet?"

"Right down the middle," the ump replied.

They played like that until past midnight, men appearing and disappearing out of the gloom like soldiers on a battlefield. The Preacher was beyond speech. He crouched low to the ground behind the plate like he was waiting for a mortar shell to hit. His breathing was heavy and audible. Spitz could hear his raspy breath all the way out at short. On the mound for the All-Stars, Rube got rattled and started walking batters. Calling time, Spitz trotted in to calm him down. "I can't see a goddamn thing," Rube complained.

Spitz turned to look at home plate. "Do you see that lamp on the batter's head?"

"Yup."

"Aim three feet lower than that and a foot to the left."

It was no use. Once Rube was rattled, as everybody knew, there was no way to calm him down. His fastballs went over the chicken wire backstop. His curve balls skittered in the sand. Batters walked to first and then scrambled around the base paths at will. Even if he had been able to see, the Preacher was in no shape to throw them out. At quarter after twelve, the score was 11-10 for the home team. It was only the sixth inning. The umpire stepped gingerly on to the field. "I'm callin this game for the lateness of the hour."

Eddie was up one side of him and down the other. "For the lateness of the hour!" he shouted. "It's been pitch-dark these past two hours."

"It's after midnight," the umpire said back. "There's been a midnight curfew in this town ever since the miners' strike. Do you want that I should break the law?"

Spitz watched as the home team vacated the field, their shoulders slumped again as though they had forgotten the game altogether the moment it was finished. He saw the headlamps glancing off squat houses as the miners made their way home. The automobiles too started up and meandered down darkened streets. Horse-drawn buggies evaporated quietly into the gloom. Soon coal-oil lamps began to flicker in the windows of the houses, and Spitz could smell the homey odor of chimney smoke. He could taste the smoke in the back of his throat. It tasted halfway between a good strong cigarette and a mouthful of gasoline. He sidled up to the Preacher, who was trembling by the backstop. "Goddamn poor sports," Spitz muttered, putting an arm around the Preacher and escorting him to the bus.

The Preacher was back to a semblance of his former self by morning, after a fitful sleep. He climbed into the driver's seat when breakfast was done. "This pop-stand gives me the heebie jeebies," he said. "I ain't too sad to leave it." He fired up the dull blue beast and down the road they headed.

There were almost no turns in the highway between Estevan and Regina, the treeless prairie flat and alkaline on both sides of the bus. It looked to Spitz like a land that had been poisoned by the very people who lived upon it, tilled to dust and dry as a popcorn fart. He lost interest in the landscape somewhere after Weyburn, pulled a tattered piece of paper from his shirt pocket and began to read.

It was a letter from Gwendolyn, a girl he'd known from his boyhood back in the Smoky Mountains. He'd told her, when he was fourteen years old, that he was going to marry her someday. Life got in the way of that, and someday never came. She had been bright as a new penny back then and for many summers afterwards, but who knew what had happened to her in the five years since Spitz had seen her last? She could be living in a big white house by now, Spitz thought, with a lawyer husband and a brood of kids. Spitz hadn't asked her to wait for him. How could he have? Ask a girl to wait for a man who traipsed around the countryside in the back of a bus, throwing horsehide and swinging lumber for a living? It would have been unconscionable.

Printed carefully with a lead pencil on yellowing paper, the letter was dated January 5, 1930. Gwendolyn had not attended school long enough to learn the art of cursive writing. "I hope you are still receiving my correspondence," it said, the print legible and child-like, "and that you still think fondly of your poor Gwendolyn. I have written faithfully, but there is never an answer. I hope you have not forgotten me." Spitz had not forgotten her, and he would never forget her. She was his one true thing in a world full of half-truths and lies, and yet he could not bring himself to respond to her letter. He had lost his innocence somewhere along the way, and he could not face her in this state of debasement. His life had become a constant searching for the thing he had lost. He carried his longing for her deep in his abdomen like the emptiness of death in a burned-out world. Probably out of boredom, Ray began to play his harmonica at that moment, and Spitz's eyes swam in tears.

The wind had come up by the time they arrived at the baseball field in Regina. Back in the days when he was still pitching, Spitz had always liked the wind in his face. His junk worked better in a brisk wind. His fader faded faster, and his spitball dipped and dived. He could really bring the magic on a windy day. This wind was different, though, bitter, destroying, like the roar of the ovens in a crematorium. Fast Eddie, who was starting that day, didn't care for the wind. It took a few miles an hour off his fastball, and his curveball wasn't worth a damn at the best of times. Eddie warmed up on the sidelines and grumbled. Nothing was good enough for him, not the weather, not the city with its smelly slough, not the ball diamond he was about to play on.

One spectator came early to watch the All-Stars practice. She was a tall lady in a red dress and a pillbox hat. Her hair was coiled in bright red ringlets, and her lipstick was a shade that movie stars wore. She sat behind the visitors' bench and keenly observed the practice. Fifteen minutes before the game was scheduled to begin, Betty could be seen clutching the chain link fence and talking to the tall lady. There was something in Betty's posture that made it clear she was talking to an old friend. It was in the way she toed the fence with her cleated foot and in the way her hips bent forward toward the lady on the other side. They chattered happily. Spitz thought to himself that it was the first time he'd ever seen Betty when she was truly happy.

Leaving the conversation reluctantly, Betty came back out on the field. "I've got us a right fielder if you want her," she said to the Preacher.

"Can she play?"

"She was a Bloomer Girl back in Chicago with me," Betty replied. "Could play pretty good back then."

The Preacher turned and sized up the lady in the red dress for a moment. "What's her name?"

"Edna. Edna Milford." There was something about how Betty said the name that made the Preacher aware of how special she was.

"Sure she can come and play," he said. "This game'll be her try-out."

Edna Milford could play all right. She went four-for-four at the plate, slapping base hits to right, left, and center. Her red dress fluttering in the stiff, hot wind, she ran the bases like a pro, even sliding into home on a close play, one hand modestly pulling at the hem of her dress to avoid public embarrassment. She played right field like a dream, tracking down one fly ball near the foul line and then throwing the runner out in a close play at home.

After the game, the Preacher said to her, "Edna, why don't you stay with the team for the rest of the tour?"

Betty spoke up in Edna's stead. "Edna's stayin put right here," she said, "and so am I."

This was news to the Preacher. "Woah, woah, woah," he said. "Now hold on just one cotton-pickin minute, Betty. You signed a contract to stay with this team for the duration of the tour."

Betty had hard blue steel somewhere near the core of her soul, and it showed up at that moment. "That contract isn't worth the paper it's written on," she replied, "and you know it. We were promised five dollars a game, cash on the barrelhead. And that hasn't exactly panned out, has it?"

The Preacher was starting to get angry, pointing a stubby finger in Betty's pretty face. "You can't blame me fer acts of God," he snarled. "Ya can't blame me if a dust storm comes up and people pay with chickens."

Betty was unmoved. "I'm not blamin you or anybody," she said. "I'm just quittin the team."

"Well, how are we gonna play when we're down to seven?" The Preacher suddenly looked a hundred years old.

"You'll find a way," Betty said quietly. "You always do."

Betty said her goodbyes as she was on the bus, packing her bags. "I'm gonna miss you, Spitzy," she said. "You were a good friend to me."

Spitz stood in the aisle, toying with the leather lacing on his glove. "I'm gonna miss you too, Sis."

"I hope one day you'll find the peace you're lookin for," she said.

"I hope you find that too."

Rube climbed onto the bus just as Betty was leaving. "Aw Betty," he bawled from the front near the driver's seat, "I thought we had a thang."

Betty smiled. "I hate to disappoint you, Rube," she said, "but you never had a fighting chance with me."

"Aw Betty," he moaned, "can't you jus' leave me knowin that we had a great love affair? Can't you leave me with that?"

"That would be a lie," Betty said. "And I don't traffic in lies no more." She collected some lipstick and pancake off the seat and threw it into her makeup box. "I sure won't miss these chickens either," she said as she walked past Rube and off the bus.

Edna was waiting for her behind the bleachers. Arm in arm, they strolled out of the ballpark like society women on a shopping spree. Spitz had never seen Betty happier. The Preacher watched her go, and then he climbed aboard the bus.

"Ya gotta hand it to Betty," he said. "She goes after what she wants."

Rube sat like a blubbering, lumpen baby in his seat. "I thought she wanted me."

"Oh, shut up, Rube," the Preacher growled. "She never wanted you or any man."

Rube shook his head sadly. "No. No, I guess not."

"If it's any consolation to ya," the Preacher added, "she's damned in the eyes of the Lord."

"She ain't damned any more than the rest of us," Spitz said.

The Preacher looked at him sternly. "You know what the Good Book says about that kind of perversion. You know what it says about Sodom and Gomorrah."

"She's no more damned than the rest of us," Spitz repeated, and the Preacher knew better than to argue.

10. Tornado

They parked in the shadow of a hotel called The Empire, to stay out of the wind. So furious was the tumult that the windows of the bus had to remain closed. It was sweltering inside. The bus rocked and swayed with the sharp gusts, and the chickens grumbled all night long from the back seats.

At sunrise, Spitz awoke and went for his usual morning walk. His eyes were welded almost shut with sleep or the lack of it, and he rubbed them incessantly as he walked down McIntyre Street. The wind had died down completely. There was a curious stillness in the air, the kind of stillness that Spitz had come to recognize as a prelude to something. He couldn't be sure, though, what the stillness presaged. Sometimes stillness was a good thing, the harbinger of a cheery day. At other times, it was a big white dog staring you in the eye. It was early morning, and no other soul had ventured out onto the streets.

Off to the south, there was a grey formation in the sky. At first, Spitz thought it was a massive flock of crows, mangy birds cackling at the fate of man. Perhaps they were congregating over the city dump. As it approached, the cloud of crows became something more heinous. Spitz felt the first blast of an angry, oven-heated wind and recognized that the tornado was carrying with it broken lumber and sharded glass. The hot confusion swirled toward him. Spitz broke into a run, but it was too late. He dove into a stairwell at the back of the Empire and clung to the iron door handles as the tornado surged past. The brutal wind grabbed at the cloth of his trousers, attempting to yank him from his hiding place. Above him, high in the eye of the storm, an old man, oblivious to the fact that he was in midair, was grasping a doorknob and the door still intact. Spitz saw a cow flying over the moon, bellowing for his salt block and his cud. He saw an old Model T, driverless, careening through the sky. He saw a storm of lumber and glass coming at him, and then he was inside a rock polisher, tumbled hard and smooth in its workings. He blacked out before the tornado had done its worst.

When he came to again, Spitz was lying in a street that was unrecognizable, strewn with upset automobiles and branches of trees. His ears were ringing with the faint hum of a gunshot fired too close. There was a man kneeling beside him. His lips were moving, and his expression was anxious. Spitz shook his head. The man's lips kept moving. After a moment, Spitz began to recover his senses. "Can you hear me?" the man yelled.

There was blood running down Spitz's face, replacing the sleep that had been in his eyes. He could see, through the blood, that the man was wearing a suit. "Are you a doctor?" he asked.

The man was wiping blood away from Spitz's forehead with a white handkerchief. "No," he said, "I'm a dentist. All the doctors are busy elsewhere."

"I got this tooth that needs to be pulled," Spitz said.

"That'll have to wait for another time," the dentist replied. "Let's get you patched up first." He helped Spitz to a sitting position. Other bodies were lying in the street, limbs akimbo. Some of them weren't moving. Spitz could see the mangled frame of a woman a hundred feet away. Her legs were splayed at an awkward angle, and the garments had been torn from her body.

"Why don't you help that lady first?" he asked the man.

"That lady is beyond help, I'm afraid."

"Well, cover her up, at least," Spitz said, a sudden anger rising. "We ain't animals."

The dentist didn't reply. He was busy wrapping a length of gauze around Spitz's forehead.

Miraculously the bus was still standing where it had been parked the night before. Tall buildings on both sides of the vehicle had protected it from the tornado. The bus didn't look too much worse for the wear either, but by then it was so beaten up and battered that it could hardly look much worse.

The chickens were chucking gregariously, no doubt congratulating one another for surviving the storm, when Spitz climbed on the bus. His teammates were sitting on the bench seats, wide-eyed and dazed, as the Preacher, standing near the driver's seat at the front of the bus, held forth on the evils of the night before. "It is the beginning of the end!" he exclaimed. "The apocalypse is upon us! We are scourged and punished for our past sins! Debauchery and greed!" The Preacher stretched one arm toward the roof of the bus and quoted scripture. "I looked, and behold, a pale horse; and he who sat on it had the name Death; and Hades was following him. Authority was given to them over a fourth of the earth, to kill with sword and with famine and with pestilence and by the wild beasts of the earth."

Spitz made his way up the aisle toward his seat. Under the gauze bandage that the dentist had applied, Spitz's head was pounding. He sat down and listened to the end of the Preacher's tirade. Then he held up his hand.

"Yes? What?" the Preacher said.

"When are we leavin this burg?"

They rolled into Moose Jaw two hours later. Cops were stationed every hundred yards or so along Railway Avenue, guarding the tracks and the boxcars that rested upon them. These policemen weren't Mounties in their scarlet regalia. They were mountainous thugs, hired by the railway for their size and their brutality. Stone-faced they watched as unemployed men milled about on the street, some with placards exhorting governments to do something. Spitz could see that the protesters were not run-of-the-mill hobos. They wore ragged baggy trousers and poor-boy caps, but they were fresh-faced and lithe, some of them skinny. Many of them looked to be in their twenties.

The Preacher parked the bus behind the grandstand at the baseball field. Spitz and his teammates disembarked. They inspected the visitors' dugout. The infield was grass, but the grass had long since turned brown.

The home team had the temerity to call themselves All-Stars, showing no deference for the Appalachians. They stretched on the outfield grass with the word "ALL-STARS" splashed across their chests in letters larger than the Appalachians sported. The Moose Jaw coach, a short man who called himself Hilton, observed the lacerations on Spitz's face as the umpire was going over ground rules. "Looks like you were talkin when you shoulda been fightin," Hilton said.

Spitz liked him even less after that.

It was Rube's turn to pitch that afternoon, but the two-man rotation was beginning to wear on him. He complained long and woefully about the soreness in his elbow. The Preacher started ragging on Spitz. "When are you gonna come outta this blue funk and pitch again?" he asked.

"Never."

"Ya can't keep carryin the torch."

"I'm done with pitchin," Spitz replied.

"If a horse bucks you off," the Preacher said, "the only way to escape the fear and embarrassment is to get back on him."

The bleachers were full that afternoon even though a major disturbance was building up at the railway tracks. The citizens of Moose Jaw seemed to love baseball. Old ladies in gingham dresses sat in the stands, knitting and crocheting between pitches. Barefooted urchins ran about between the backstop and the seats, collecting foul balls and turning them in for the price of a nickel. Farmers, their coveralls spattered with oil and dirt, smoked cigarettes and analyzed the play. Directly behind home plate, three rows up, sat a pair of men in spiffy suits and fedoras. He couldn't be sure, but Spitz thought one of those men was the same guy who'd accosted them at the restaurant parking lot back in North Dakota. For a moment, Spitz wondered how two of Capone's henchmen could get into the country so easily, but then he remembered how easy his own crossing had been.

Luckily no women flashed their legs at Rube that afternoon. Nobody brought puppy dogs or shiny objects into the stands. Rube pitched a solid game from start to finish, and the Appalachians, playing with seven men, were scraping out a win. Then, in the bottom of the eighth inning, a resounding thunderclap was heard. A sulfurous haze rose from the trainyards and then a barrage of shouting. A man, standing at the top of the grandstand, shouted, "They've opened fire down there!" The crowd evacuated hurriedly, trampling over one another, and headed southward down the avenue.

The ball players followed, curious to witness the unfolding spectacle. Spitz saw a pack of rioters descend upon a railway policeman, beating him senseless with his own baton.

Others dragged their fallen comrades off the street, administering whatever medical aid they could muster. Oblivious to danger, the Child Prodigy waded into the fray, exhorting the homeless men to put away their animosities. "Friends!" he shouted. "Put up! And reason coldly of your differences!" In payment for his soliloquy, he was almost hit by an errant bullet that whizzed so close by his misshapen head that he could feel the heat of it. He found his way back to where the rest of the Appalachians stood, around the corner of a brick building. The Preacher's hands were shaking perceptibly. "Let's get back on the bus," the Prodigy said. "This fucking country is going to the dogs." The pitched battle went on for half an hour, when the Mounties arrived and fired live ordnance into a crowd of protesters. At last, the young men in poor-boy hats were quelled. They retreated up the street and disappeared down alleys and into derelict buildings.

When they were safely on the bus, the Child Prodigy called the roll because the Preacher was incapacitated. "Spitzy."

"Yeah."

"Ray."

"He's here," said Spitz.

"Clarence."

"Yup."

"Eddie."

There was no response.

"Eddie? Where the fuck's Eddie?"

Rube spoke up. "I saw him talkin to some guys in suits."

"When?"

"Just as we was leavin the ballpark."

"We'd better find him fast!" the Prodigy said. He turned to the Preacher. "You in any shape to drive?"

The Preacher stared back blankly.

Throwing himself into the driver's seat, the Prodigy fired up the engine. Tires spinning as the bus careened out of the parking lot, the Prodigy navigated down Caribou Street, his head barely above the steering wheel, his right leg stretched to reach the gas pedal. He turned left on Main, slowing for every alley, hoping to catch a glimpse of Eddie along the way. He patrolled like that for about an hour, passing conclaves of bedraggled and wounded protesters and men and women walking briskly toward their homes. There was no sign of Eddie.

They were about ready to give up the search when Clarence, peering out his window, shouted, "I think that's him!"

"Where?" the Prodigy shouted back.

"Up ahead! Goin into that laundry!"

Sure enough, as Spitz could see, Eddie was entering the laundry, still in his ball uniform, a hoodlum on either side of him. The Prodigy slammed on the brakes, and the players disembarked, sprinting down the sidewalk to the laundry's front door. Trying to conceal his trusty Colt .45 in the folds of his jersey, the Prodigy was slower than the rest.

"Laundry closed!" shouted an old Chinese man as they entered. He was wearing a grey suit and a skull cap.

"We saw some men come in here," Spitz replied.

"Laundry closed!" the old man repeated, more forcefully.

Spitz took a step toward the back room. The laundryman stood in his way. "What's in there?" Spitz asked.

"Laundry closed!"

Spitz shoved the old man to the floor and scrambled over him into the back room. The others followed. There was a massive washtub in the room, and a young worker was stirring the clothing in the tub with a wooden paddle. The young worker did not bother to impede their progress. Perhaps he was afraid of deportation. Spitz could see a curtained exit at the far end of the room, and he went to inspect. It was a cribbed vertical shaft, accessible by a wooden ladder that led down into the darkness.

As he stepped down the ladder into the shaft, Spitz heard the echo of muffled voices, but he could not discern the direction from which they came. The shaft communicated with two tunnels that led in opposite directions. There was a rude haphazard string of incandescent bulbs that flickered in both directions, providing adequate lighting in the immediate vicinity of each bulb but also many dark shadows elsewhere. The tunnel smelled of urine and laundry soap.

When the rest of the team had also descended the ladder, they stood quietly, listening again. The muffled voices seemed to emanate from both directions, and they seemed to be getting further away. "You totin, Rube?" the Child Prodigy asked in a whisper.

"I never leave home without it," Rube said, offering a glimpse of his shiny revolver.

"You and Ray and Spitz head off that away," the Prodigy said, pointing down the tunnel toward the right. "I'll take Clarence and the Preacher, and we'll go in the opposite direction."

Spitz and Ray and Rube rushed down the passageway on the right, stopping occasionally when voices could be heard. After a while, it was difficult to discern whether the voices belonged to Fast Eddie and his abductors or to the Prodigy and his crew. The tunnel was cold and damp, with chalky calcifications on its walls that looked in the semi-darkness like prehistoric art. Occasionally Spitz could see the rough lead casings of sewage pipes above and beside him. He could hear the tires of cars rumbling on the streets above. The tunnel narrowed and, again, branched off in two directions. Rube turned to Spitz. "You okay waitin here while I take a look down thataway?"

Spitz said yeah, and Rube disappeared down the tunnel. They waited a good long time. The flicker of the incandescent lights became more pronounced. Ray held on to the sleeve of Spitz's thick woolen sweatshirt. "I'm ascared, Spitzy," he said when the lights flickered out and did not come back on again.

"No need to be scared," Spitz assured him. "Just think of yer home down there in California."

This seemed to placate Ray. "I will," he replied. "I'll think of them tall redwoods, standing like guards overtop of me."

"Yeah," Spitz whispered, "you think of the redwoods."

A gunshot rang out, too close for comfort, and Spitz decided to move. "Keep ahold of my arm," he said to Ray. They proceeded down the narrow tunnel to the right. Its odors were more caustic now, gunpowder and methane gas. It walls were sometimes so close together that both men had to turn sideways and scrunch up their bodies to continue. The ceiling slumped so low that Spitz found himself hunched over to avoid bumping his head on the cribbing. Tracing their way along clammy walls, they heard voices up ahead, this time clearer than before. Spitz didn't recognize the first voice. "So you thought you could double-cross

Capone and get away with it?" The voice echoed eerily down the passageway.

Spitz recognized the second voice. It was Eddie's. "I didn't think to double-cross anybody."

"I'm ascared, Spitzy," Ray said again, a little too loud.

Spitz turned, clasping Ray's shoulders in his hands and looking him in the eye as best he could in that dark place. "It's gonna be all right, Ray," he whispered, more harsh and guttural than he intended. "You jus' wait right here. I'll come back fer you in a minute or two."

"I'll wait here," Ray said.

"And don't move."

"No. I won't move."

Spitz tore a splintered chunk of cribbing off the side of the tunnel, wielding it in front of him like a baseball bat. He figured the element of surprise was on his side, that he could sneak up on the gangster with a rearward action and clout him over the head. Scrambling down the tunnel alone in the direction of the voices, Spitz thought how badly he needed a drink. If he could only have a drink, he thought, order would be restored and the world would be righted again. The tunnel twisted and turned, narrowed and widened. There was another fork and then another. Spitz recoiled when he heard more gunshots, crowning himself on a beam that protruded above him. The echo of the gunshots reverberated through the tunnel like the Voice of God. Concussed and half-senseless, Spitz rushed forward, without sense of direction, arriving at last in an open area where the light was better. He could see now that the chunk of cribbing would do him no good.

Eddie was on his knees in a pool of light. Behind Eddie was a gangster, not the scar-faced man but his henchman, the burly fellow who'd accompanied him. The gangster's handgun was aimed directly at the back of Eddie's head. Behind the gangster was the Child Prodigy. The barrel of the Prodigy's Colt .45 was pressed deep into the crack of the gangster's ass, so deep that the gangster was up on his tiptoes, like he was in the middle of a sad hemorrhoid examination. Rube stood off to one side, his shiny pistol pointed at the gangster's temple. Clarence was pasted against a clammy wall, and the Preacher stood some distance away, his anxious face all but invisible in the semi-darkness.

"There don't gotta be no killin," the Prodigy said, as calmly as he could. "Just put the gun down and we'll all walk away as if nothin happened."

"You put your gun down first," the burly gangster replied. "And then we'll talk."

"I'd stand a little more still if I was you," the Prodigy said. "This gun's got a hair trigger."

"So does mine," the gangster replied.

From where he was standing, Spitz could see a glimmer of a grin on the gangster's lips, the kind of delirious grin that precedes an act of pure madness. He saw the man begin to pull the trigger, saw Eddie squeeze his eyes shut in preparation, and then the report of another gun perforated Spitz's eardrums. He waited for Eddie to fall face forward on the damp dirt. He waited, but Eddie didn't topple. Still kneeling there, Eddie opened his eyes wide, afraid to breathe. The gangster's eyes were wide too. He teetered for a moment and then fell forward, landing beside Eddie in the dirt.

They stayed like that in the gloom of the tunnel for a long time, a grotesque tableau of the angry spirit of the age. Finally, the Prodigy broke the silence. "You okay, Eddie?"

Eddie nodded his head.

"You okay, Spitz?"

"Yeah, I'm fine," Spitz said. And then he vomited.

The Prodigy peered down at the corpse. "He had it comin."

"He surely did," Clarence added, without a shred of remorse.

"Where's the other guy?" Rube asked.

"He's down here somewhere," the Preacher said, his voice still shaky. "We'd best get out of here."

11. Tunnels

They were almost back at the Chinese laundry when Spitz remembered Ray.

"Christ!" the Prodigy said. "D'you mean we gotta go back in there!"

"I can go it alone," Spitz replied.

The Prodigy thought it over. "You'll get yourself killed down there," he said. "There's safety in numbers." He turned to Clarence. "You take Eddie and the Preacher back to the bus. We'll be out in a few minutes."

Clarence, Eddie, and the Preacher climbed the ladder and disappeared into the Chinese laundry. Spitz, Rube, and the Prodigy hurried down the underground corridors again. Spitz tried to retrace his steps. He remembered the sweaty sewage pipes and the street noises above one of the passages. They came to the place where the tunnel branched off and narrowed. "Which way now?" the Prodigy asked.

"I ain't sure."

The Prodigy pointed with the barrel of his gun. "You two go thataway. I'll go this."

Then it was Rube and Spitz, hurrying together down a tunnel that seemed unfamiliar. The lights flickered and went out. Spitz paused, afraid of hitting his head again on the low-hanging cribbing. The lights did not come back on. "We got to keep goin," Spitz whispered at last. "Ray's in here somewhere."

"You lead and I'll follow," Rube replied.

Spitz could hear nothing but his own belabored breathing and the pounding of his heart as he edged his way down the dark corridor. There was another turn and then another. The darkness was complete and unabating. It surrounded and invaded him. Spitz could not see his own creased and sweating hand before his eyes. He imagined that death was something like this. "Rube," he whispered. "You still there?"

Rube did not answer.

"Rube? Rube?"

He heard a voice from somewhere. “Spitzy!” On all fours now, Spitz scrambled down the tunnel toward the voice. “Spitzy!” It was Ray’s voice, muffled, close and yet far away.

“Keep talkin, Ray!” Spitz shouted. “I’ll find you.” He could hear Ray’s voice but, as he moved toward it, the voice seemed to recede in the distance. “Keep talkin!” He scurried further along the darkened corridor, feeling his way along the jagged, clammy walls with his hands. He found another passageway off to the left, one that he could stand erect in. He could hear Ray’s voice again, this time clearer. Stepping gingerly down the pitch-dark passageway, Spitz felt the planking beneath his feet give way.

Then he was falling, falling hard into a deep chasm. Clutching at the rocks or the bricks or whatever on the sides of the chasm, he could not get a purchase. He hit bottom with a thud, his already once-concussed noggin clanging off a rock or a brick or something. The last thing he saw, before passing out, was an old man dressed all in white linen, smoking a corncob pipe.

There was light at the bottom of the chasm, but how could there be? It didn’t seem right. Spitz tried to sit up. His head was pounding. The old man was still there with him, perched on a small pile of bricks. They seemed to be at the bottom of a dry cistern. “You might want to stay still for a while,” the old man said to Spitz.

“Who are you?” Spitz’s head hurt when he spoke.

“No man and every man,” the old man said.

Spitz was wary, but the old man seemed kinder than before. “What are you doing here?”

“I came to give you this,” the old man said. He reached into the pocket of his waistcoat and produced a calling card.

“What is it?”

“It’s your salvation,” the old man replied. “A man can run fast and far, but he cannot escape himself.”

Spitz held out his hand to accept the calling card, but the effort was too great. His eyes swam, and he passed out again, still falling, falling deeply and endlessly toward the center of the earth.

He hit bottom a second time, and then he dreamed horrifically of the last pitch he ever threw in the major leagues.

The lights were back on when Spitz awoke a second time. The old man was nowhere to be seen. Spitz could hear the lulling sounds of a harmonica. The tune was "Old Black Joe," and there was something in the playing of it that was quaint and homey. Memories of village hall dances, back in Georgia, and of his daddy playing the fiddle, floated into Spitz's consciousness. He looked up, and the light was almost blinding, but he could see Ray perched at the rim of the cistern above him, legs dangling over, blowing into his mouth harp as if he were still sitting on the bus.

Upon seeing Spitz's eyes open, Ray ceased his playing and said, "You okay, Spitzy?"

"I'm all right." Spitz's head was throbbing again.

"I found us a ladder," Ray said. "I'll slide it down to you." Ray disappeared for a moment, and then Spitz could see the bottom rungs of a wooden ladder protruding down into the hole. Once the ladder was lowered to the base of the cistern, Ray steadied it at the top. "Are you fit to climb?"

"I think so." Spitz pulled himself to a standing position, using the ladder as a crutch. Nauseous as he ascended the rungs, he trained his eyes on Ray's gentle face. When Spitz reached the top of the ladder, Ray grabbed his thick undershirt at the collar and pulled him to safety. The two men were sprawled on the rickety planks for some time while Spitz caught his breath.

"I found a way outta here," Ray said. "I can show ya."

"Did you see Rube or the Prodigy in yer travels?"

"I ain't seen them since we got off the bus," Ray replied.

"Did ya see the gangster with the scar on his face?"

"I ain't seen him either."

It was a bit like the blind leading the blind but Spitz, disoriented as he was, entrusted himself to Ray. They traversed labyrinthine tunnels together, sometimes walking through water a foot deep, sometimes turning sideways to squirm through narrow apertures. Ray led the way, holding Spitz's hand as an adult holds the hand of a toddler. "You sure you know where you're goin?" Spitz asked.

"Sure, I'm sure." Ray continued to lead, at last bringing Spitz to a rough wooden staircase. They climbed the staircase together and came to a door that was painted red. The door was not locked. They proceeded into an anteroom that was well-appointed, with plush armchairs and stained wooden walls.

Spitz could hear lively conversation coming from the next room. "Where are we?" he asked.

"Dunno," Ray said. "There's lots of women."

When they opened the next door, they were confronted with the spectacle of half-dressed women and their male clients. The women were drinking whisky in tumblers, draping their arms around the men's shoulders or sitting in their laps. Spitz could smell the whisky, and it made him thirst for a drink. This was a room that had known debauchery for some time; the whisky had soaked into the carpet and the plush chairs. The men looked to be the business elite of Moose Jaw. They were wearing expensive suits and patent leather shoes. Smoke from their cigars curled toward the ceiling and settled in a haze around them. A gramophone in the corner was playing swing music and jazz.

One of the women, a corpulent madam with a tall mast of red hair on her head, noticed Spitz and Ray as they entered. "Well, if it isn't the hardball players from down south," she said. "You boys look like you could both use a good, solid, down-to-earth lay."

"I could," Spitz said.

Ray was tugging at his sleeve. "C'mon Spitzy. We gotta vamoose." Spitz followed him to the door.

"You ain't stayin?" the red-haired madam asked.

Spitz shrugged his shoulders. "You heard the man."

"Why'd you come here," she asked, "if you ain't planning to stay a spell?" But Ray and Spitz were already out of the room. They hurried into the foyer and found an exit. A wizened old doorman was standing there, peering through a peephole at whatever was outside. Hearing their footsteps, he turned to Spitz and Ray. "You don't wanna go out there right now."

"Oh?" Spitz replied. "Why not?"

The doorman rubbed his bristly chin. "There's cops everywhere. Musta bin some shenanigans at the laundry across the street."

"We gotta be somewhere fast," Spitz said.

"I'll show you out the back." The aged doorman escorted them through the foyer, down a hallway and through the galley kitchen to the back door.

As the door closed behind them with a declarative thud, Spitz understood that they were in an alley and that it was a moonless night. His head was still throbbing, but he was beginning to regain his senses. He looked around at back stoops and trash cans, saw the gentle slope of the alley, and then he remembered that the railyards were at the bottom of the hill. "C'mon," he said to Ray.

"Where are we goin?"

"Just follow me."

Ten minutes later, Spitz and Ray were crouched in a door well, under the cover of darkness, watching the railyards. The place was crawling with cops, not just railway thugs but also Mounties. They were patrolling in all directions. One of the patrols stopped across the street from the building where Spitz and Ray were hiding.

"Hey!" a cop shouted. "There's two more over there!" The patrol broke into a run toward them, and Spitz and Ray burst out of the door well and started running too. "Stop, or we'll shoot!" Spitz heard the cop holler, and then there was the ping and thud of bullets ricocheting off garbage cans and lodging themselves in wooden walls. Spitz and Ray sprinted hard to get away, zigging and zagging down streets and alleys, until the shooting stopped and the patrol had apparently lost interest.

They were hiding between two parked cars on Caribou Street when Spitz saw the team bus speeding toward them. He ran into the street and waved his arms. The bus skidded to a stop, and the Preacher, newly recovered from the delirium of the tunnels, threw open the door. "You boys are just in time," he said as Spitz pushed Ray up the steps and scrambled in behind. "We're just about to leave this shit-hole."

Spitz stopped at the top of the steps and surveyed the seats. Rube and the Prodigy were sitting there with the rest of the players. "You lost us in the tunnel," the Prodigy explained. "Knew we'd see you back here eventually."

There was little time for further chitchat. The Preacher tromped on the foot-feed, anxious to put Moose Jaw and its tunnels and its railyards and its protesters and its cops in his rear-view mirror. Five minutes later, they were out of town and speeding through the dark countryside.

12. A Plague of Locusts

They played the next day in a town called Davidson. It was a small place with little to recommend it, halfway between Moose Jaw and Saskatoon, smack-dab in the middle of a prairie so flat and wide that you could see your wife walking out on you for three days. The fields around the town were green, unlike where they had just come from.

As Spitz was donning his uniform in preparation for the game, a grey card fluttered out of the back pocket of his flannel baseball trousers. Spitz picked up the card from the floor of the bus. He vaguely remembered seeing the card the night before, but he thought the entire incident had been a product of his concussed brain. Still feeling the effects of the concussion, he strained to read the card. It took him some time, but eventually he was able to decipher the ornate print. "Professor John Chatterwood," the card read, "332 Lincoln Avenue, Salinas, California, USA." Spitz stared at this remnant of his lost evening in the tunnels, hardly believing his own eyes. His legs were shaking, and he felt himself break into an icy sweat. When the Preacher announced that it was time to take the field, Spitz fought to regain his composure. He took a deep breath, deposited the card in his duffle bag, and finished dressing.

A jubilant farmer, who was standing behind the chicken wire backstop as the Appalachians warmed up, told Spitz that a column of rain had come through just a week earlier. "Yesiree," the farmer said, "you are in God's Country now. That rain dropped buckets on our wheat fields, and now we're lookin fer a bumper crop."

"Best not to count yer chickens before they hatch," Spitz replied. Experience had taught him that lesson well.

They played on a diamond that might have been a stubble field three days earlier. It sloped uphill toward the gravel highway that ran along the perimeter of left field. "Anything hit onto the highway or over it," the umpire said, "is a home run." The infield was ridged, as if by a harrow or a discer. It consisted of brown dirt and rocks the size of Spitz's fist. The locals had taken care to divest the place of any stone larger than that.

The Appalachians did not play well. Still shell-shocked from the night before, Fast Eddie could not find the plate until the third inning. Spitz's vision was not perfect, and ground balls took ungainly bounces off the infield stones. He was hit in the throat by one and couldn't talk above a whisper for the rest of the game. Rube, who was not seeing double, took a one-hopper off the forehead and was hesitant to get in front of anything after that. The Appalachians ended up losing 15-14. As they were shaking hands after the game, a home team player grinned and asked Spitz, "You guys were major leaguers in the recent past?"

They did get paid for the game, though, and Clarence arranged another chicken fry afterwards. He found some scrap two-by-fours near the baseball diamond, started a fire, and cooked up six more hens. Spitz and the boys ate voraciously as the sun began its slow decline in the west.

When the meal was done, Spitz and Eddie went for a walk down to the railway tracks. Eddie was unusually humble and weak of spirit. "I didn't do it, Spitzy," he said.

"Didn't do what?"

"What they said I done."

"I wouldn't blame you if you had," Spitz said. "Them owners were stiffin us left, right, and center."

"Yeah, but I didn't," Eddie repeated. "Capone's fellas asked me to throw it, but I played hard."

"I believe you."

They saw, behind a grain elevator, a threesome of hobos whooping it up, telling dirty jokes and laughing and passing a mickey around. There was a fire in the barrel in front of them. Spitz and Eddie approached the bums. They were young men in ragged clothes, possibly some of the same men they'd seen in Moose Jaw a day earlier. "Are you fellas friends or foes?" one of the hobos asked, slurring his esses.

"Friends," said Spitz.

"Have a drink then," the hobo said. He thrusted the mickey toward Spitz, and Spitz took it from him. He held the bottle at arm's length for some time, examining the amber liquid in the fading light. It looked like medicine, just the kind of medicine Spitz needed to get through the rest of this tour.

"Don't do it, Spitzy." There was urgency in Eddie's voice. He'd heard all the stories of the last few years, how Spitz had faded away in an alcoholic haze after the beaning incident. Everybody in baseball had heard those stories, and everybody had lamented the sad waste of his God-given talent. But Spitz didn't listen to Eddie. He put the bottle to his lips, tasting the first savory fumes of the whisky, and then he tipped the bottle heavenward and swallowed something that felt like warm paradise in his belly.

Spitz was drunk and laughing a half hour later. He guffawed at a joke about a Mountie and his gunnery badge. All was right in the world for the first time in a long while, but deep in his abdomen Spitz sensed that happiness was only fleeting. Eddie stood aloof and didn't drink, a wistful look on his face.

Another omen was rising out of the west, silhouetted in the drooping sun. It looked to Spitz like another dust storm at first, but the stillness that preceded most storms hadn't materialized. When Spitz looked again, the hobos had vanished, probably hiding behind the elevator annex. Spitz and Eddie watched as the low-lying cloud approached them, almost in slow motion. "What the hell is that now?" Eddie said.

"The beginning of the end," Spitz replied, half-joking.

The cloud advanced. Spitz felt the first few abrasions on his face like wads of paper blown through a straw. Then there was something crawling on him, tasting his dried sweat. He looked at Eddie, whose face was all but covered with insects. "Run!" he shouted, and the two men ran for all they were worth. A plague of locusts blacked out the sun. The sky was filled with their insatiable hunger. Spitz and Eddie ran hard toward the faint outline of the bus while the insects battered their bodies and chewed at their clothes. The bus, too, was covered with locusts by the time Spitz and Eddie arrived. The Preacher opened the door a crack, and the two men slid in sideways. To his relief, Spitz could see that Ray was safely in his seat, playing his harmonica.

"What a god-forsaken country this is," the Preacher said as Ray blew into his mouth harp and the insects smashed headlong into the side of the bus, leaving suicidal green splotches on the windows. "Just makes a fella wanna go home."

The storm of locusts subsided in the early morning hours. The Preacher walked to a gas station to ask for a pail of water, but he was told that water was in short supply. When he came back to the bus, he was toting a can of antifreeze that had cost him two dollars. He dabbed a towel in the antifreeze and rubbed the windshield as clear as he could get it. There was still a soft green haze on the glass when he was finished.

Stepping off the bus to look around, Spitz witnessed the result of the previous evening's ravages. In all directions, the fields that had been green and windswept a day earlier were now desolate and devoured to the earth. The leaves on the caragana hedges were gone. Even the quack grass that had grown along the side of the highway was mowed clean to the roots. It looked like a prairie fire had passed through, leaving the soil black, cindery, and infertile.

When he had finished washing the windshield, the Preacher urged his players to get back on the bus. "Next stop is a place called Hanley," he said. "That sounds like a sweeter place."

Just then, Eddie came off the bus, his duffle bag slung over his shoulder. "You'll have to do it without me," he said. His jaw was set like he was pitching himself out of a jam.

The Preacher was stunned. "What the hell, Eddie! We can't do it without you."

"Can't do it with me either," Eddie said. "I've brought down some fearful things upon this team."

"If you leave, we're down to six. We can't play with six guys.

"You can and you will."

The Preacher sat down on the step of the bus. "Goddamit, Eddie, let's talk this out."

"Ain't nothin to talk about."

"Just tell me what brought this on."

Eddie rested his duffle bag on the barren ground beside him. "It's bin a long time comin," he said. "I just have to go back and face my past."

"There's nothin back there for you," the Preacher said. "There's nothin back there for any of us."

"We'll see about that," said Eddie.

"Look, I believed you when you said you didn't do it." The Preacher was almost begging Eddie to stay.

"But the rest of the world don't believe me," Eddie replied, "and I mean to change that." He looked tired and twenty years older than he had looked the day before, but his jaw was still set. He picked up his duffle bag and headed toward the highway. The rest of the team watched as he held out his thumb to a passing motorist. A sedan went by and then another. He stood at the side of the road for half an hour, his teammates watching all that time, and then a pickup truck stopped to let him on. He threw his duffle into the box of the truck and climbed into the cab. The last the team saw of Eddie, he was heading south down Highway Number Eleven.

The Preacher rubbed his gnarled hand over his face. "Maybe Eddie's right," he said. "If we can play with seven guys, we can surely play with six. Rube'll pitch. Spitz will move to first. Clarence'll stay at third. Ray and the Prodigy will patrol the outfield, which won't matter a damn cuz nobody's gonna hit anything out there anyway. Any problems with that?"

Spitz could think of all sorts of problems, but he didn't have the heart to mention any of them. Neither did anyone else. They got back on the bus and headed out of town.

When they were on the highway and going north, they passed a field that had once been green with the promise of a bumper crop. A farmer was standing amidst the desiccated stocks of wheat, surveying the damage. It was the same farmer Spitz had encountered the night before, at the ballgame. He was wearing the same grey overalls and, although he stood a hundred yards away, Spitz could see the farmer's body shaking, his head bowed as he tallied the cost of God's wrath.

Hanley was little more than a village on the side of the highway, a place that looked like a stop-off on a road to somewhere else. There were maybe fifty houses in the town, a grain elevator and, oddly enough, a pretty opera house that sat on Main Street like a society matron on a barstool. Spitz wondered if anyone sang opera in this town and if anyone knew how to play baseball.

There was a commotion on the steps of the opera house as the Appalachians rolled into town. A crowd had gathered round, and a neatly besuited man with crisp pomaded hair was holding forth in front of the spectators. Strewn across the entrance to the opera house was a banner that read "Say No to Immigration." The speaker had a certain charm about him; he spoke soothingly of the values people held dear—law and order, good government, equal opportunity, the pleasures of home and hearth. "The Liberal government," he intoned, "the government of Jimmy Gardiner, has little respect for these long-held values. Where does he stand on the immigration crisis? Ladies and gentlemen, I'm here to tell you that a way of life is under threat. Imagine, if you will, a Catholic church erected just over there." He pointed to an empty expanse of prairie. "Imagine your new neighbors and their Frenchified ways. Imagine hordes of immigrants—Slavs and Scandinavians, Jews, Red Russians, and the Chinese. Imagine them marrying your sons and daughters, diluting the blood of this Great Race."

Spitz stood in the crowd and listened to the politician's spiel. It reminded him of the spiels of almost every politician he'd ever heard. The more things change, he thought, the more they stay the same. He wondered how the locals would take to Clarence. Spitz might have interrupted the politician with an objection, but he had other things on his mind. He turned to the rancher standing next to him and asked, "Where can I buy a bottle in this town?"

The rancher tipped up his cowboy hat and looked at Spitz severely. "You a cop?"

"No."

"What are you then?"

"I'm a baseball player."

"You one of them Americans?"

"Yeah."

The rancher grinned at him and pointed to another man, a lean old fellow at the edge of the gathering. "Go talk to Samuel over there. He'll set you up."

"Thanks." Spitz went and talked to the lean old man who did, indeed, set him up. They went together to the old man's rickety house where, for a mere dollar, Spitz was able to purchase a mason jar full of clear corn liquor. He downed the home brew right there on the old man's back porch, and then he straightened himself up and strode like a king to the baseball field.

"Where you bin?" the Preacher asked Spitz as he was tying the laces of his cleats.

"Bin to see a man about a horse," Spitz replied breezily, not bothering to look the Preacher in the eye.

"Well, I hope yer fit to play."

The Preacher had every right to be concerned, having only six players at his disposal. Ray and the Child Prodigy patrolled the outfield. As planned, Spitz played on the right side of the infield. Clarence moved to third. Rube was pitching, and the Preacher caught.

When the game started, Rube seemed distracted on the mound. His knuckle slurve wasn't working. It floated to the plate like a log in the River of Time, and the Hanley boys were hitting him hard. By the end of the second inning, Spitz became aware of how powerful the old man's corn liquor really was. He missed a can of corn pop fly in the third, the ball dropping beside him like a duck shot out of the air. In the fourth inning, a routine grounder went bounding between his legs. When the inning was over, Rube threw his glove hard into the dirt and plopped his burly carcass on the slivery pine bench. "Did you silly fuckers forget how to play this here game?" he muttered.

Spitz heard him and took exception to the remark. "Maybe if you could put the ball on a corner once in a while, we wouldn't be so active on the field."

"And maybe," Rube replied, "if you weren't ascared of pitchin, you could take your turn."

On a normal day, Spitz would have let this slide. Somehow, though, this wasn't a normal day. He got to his feet, unsteadily. "Maybe if you could keep your mind on what you're doing," he said, "you'd still be playin in the show."

Rube stood up too. "And maybe if you hadn't thrown that beanball—" He didn't get more than that out. Spitz cocked his arm and swung at the big man as hard as he could. Rube slipped the punch and came back with a haymaker of his own. The last sights Spitz remembered seeing were the wide prairie sky reeling above him, the look of horror on Ray's face, and the ground rising up to meet him.

13. Temperance

They were all on the bus, riding into Saskatoon, when Spitz came to. His head hurt something terrible as the vehicle rumbled over uneven gravel. "What happened?" he said to Clarence. "Did we win?"

Clarence looked at him piteously. "We couldn't finish the game," he said. "Umpire told us he wouldn't officiate if teammates were gonna be fightin amongst themselves."

Spitz turned and looked at Rube. He was staring morosely out the window on his side of the bus, not at all his normal self. Ray was blowing into his harmonica, as if playing could blow the trouble away. Spitz got up, supporting himself on the back of the seat. "I'm sorry fer what I said and done," he told Rube. "It was my fault." Ray stopped playing. The bus was quiet except for the rumble of the tread bare tires along the road.

Rube didn't even bother to look at Spitz. "Jus' take a seat," he said. "We'll talk about it some other time."

There was a team meeting in Saskatoon the next morning. The six remaining members of the Appalachian All-Stars sat on the bus outside Cairns Field and discussed their future. "We can't have no more fightin amongst ourselves," the Preacher said from the front of the bus. "If we ain't got each other's backs, we ain't got no team."

"When are we gonna get paid again?" Clarence asked. "I ain't seen a pay cheque since we crossed the border."

The Preacher took a deep breath. "You know as well as I do that a person can't insure against Acts of God. We had us a tornado and a locust storm. We've seen riots and teams that refused to honor their contracts. You can't insure against those things."

Rube was staring down at the dirty floor of the bus. "How we gonna eat if this keeps up?"

"We still got half a dozen chickens," the Preacher replied, gesturing to the sleepy birds at the back of the bus. "That'll hold us fer a while." The hens chucked and warbled.

"I'm sick of eatin chicken," Rube muttered. "If I eat another chicken, I'm likely to sprout feathers."

There was a moment's pause, and then the Preacher offered a suggestion. "There's the river over there," he said, pointing. "I'm thinkin what this city needs is a good old-fashioned baptism."

Spitz found out too late that Saskatoon was a temperance city. There were no public houses on one side of the river, and Spitz had not had the foresight to ask the old gentleman in Hanley for a second bottle of hooch. He found himself wandering through the city's downtown that afternoon, looking aimlessly for something there was little hope of finding.

His lips dry and his body aching, he sat down in a Chinese restaurant and tried a trick that had worked for him in Cleveland several years earlier. "I'd like a cup of yer special green tea," he said to the young waiter. He placed an American greenback on the table. "Make sure it's yer special tea."

"You police?" the waiter asked, in broken English.

"I ain't no cop," Spitz said. He held his arms out so that the waiter could have full view of him. "No badge, no gun."

"Perhaps you might like to visit our tearoom," the waiter said.

He escorted Spitz through the kitchen of the restaurant, sweaty with the busy work of several cooks, and from there through a curtain and down a flight of ramshackle stairs. The restaurant's cellar had none of the charm of its above ground level; there were no colorful Chinese lanterns or red tablecloths or paintings of junks in harbors. The cellar was not well lit, but Spitz could see dirt walls. Some old men were playing a game that looked like dominos at a table under a bare light bulb.

There was a partition crafted out of portable screens in one corner of the cellar, and Spitz followed the waiter to the other side of the partition. A pretty woman was seated near a steel cot. The only splashes of color were the red dress she wore and the brass bracelets on her wrists. She motioned to Spitz to sit on the ratty mattress. The springs of the cot creaked wearily under his weight. On a table nearby was a long wooden pipe and an oil lamp. It looked like the lamp of a genie. "No," Spitz said. "I only wanted whisky."

The woman pushed him down again on the cot. She warmed the long pipe over the lamp's bright flame and then pressed the open end of the pipe into Spitz's mouth. He inhaled the pungent smoke and exhaled it in a coil that rose to the ceiling. He decided not to resist further. He felt his troubles melting away, rising heavenward with the smoke, and then he was rising heavenward with them. Up and up he went, through the ceiling above him and the ceiling above that. He was floating over the city and its mighty river, floating over the ball diamond and the traffic on the streets. It all seemed small and petty to him then. The travails of the world were momentary.

He found himself in an apple orchard, blossoms fragrant in the afternoon heat. The old man was sitting in the orchard. He was still dressed in the white suit and the high-collared shirt. His hair and his moustache were white and unkempt. His skin was pastier than before, almost waxy, and he sat with the stillness of a statue. The old man's eyes were lifeless when he turned to look at Spitz. "It's time," the old man said. "It's time to bring him home."

And then the pretty woman was on top of Spitz with her red dress hiked up to her waist and her long graceful arms performing a kind of dance and her brass bracelets chiming in his ears and then he touched her breasts and she arched her back and when she was done Spitz saw her reach into his wallet and take whatever cash remained and then she got up and left and the oil lamp flickered beside the bed and then he slept.

When Spitz woke up, he searched in his trouser pockets for the watch Gwendolyn had given him. He was relieved to find that the watch had not been stolen. It was past seven o'clock. The ball game had already started. Woozily he got to his feet, buttoned his shirt. He heard footfalls on the floor above him, voices rising in crescendo. The woman had gone, but the light of the oil lamp still burned bright. Spitz was nauseous for a moment.

He looked away from the lamp. He thought he might puke. Something seemed to explode inside his head. His knees buckled, and he fell face forward onto the mattress. He slept like an angel after that and, when he awoke again, the oil lamp had gone out and there was a stillness in the room above.

It was early the next morning when Spitz straggled back to the bus. There was some movement in the parking lot of the baseball field when he arrived. The cinders of the campfire were just going out. Ray and the Child Prodigy were washing metal dishes in buckets of river water. Rube and Clarence were swanning around the campsite in dark suits. As Spitz arrived, the Preacher was descending the steps of the bus. He was wearing his flowing white liturgical gown. Spitz approached him sheepishly. "You missed the game," the Preacher said. "I'll have to dock your pay."

"Sorry," Spitz offered, "I lost track of time."

"Don't let it happen again." The Preacher had little else to say. He strode across the parking lot and headed east toward the river.

Spitz approached Ray and the Child Prodigy, who were emptying pails of dishwater into the gravel. "What's goin on?"

"The Preacher needed to make some money," the Prodigy said, "to git us paid. So he issued an invitation to come be baptized last night at the ball game."

"And the baptism's startin now?"

The Prodigy nodded. "Better git into yer suit if you wanna help."

Spitz hurried on to the bus and pulled his wrinkled suit out of his duffle bag. The chickens watched him, from their roosts in the back, with jaundiced eyeballs. He was still a little groggy as he was donning the suit, and he tied his shoes in an odd bow. When he was dressed and looking respectable, he joined the others out in the lot, and they headed together down to the riverbank. Rube, Ray, and the Child Prodigy were carrying heavy wooden collection plates. "How'd we do in the game last night?" Spitz asked.

"We lost," Rube said. "Pretty darn hard to win when yer playin with five guys."

When they arrived at the riverbank, the Preacher was already standing waist-deep in the fast-moving water. There was a large congregation of people on the bank and more coming down through the thicket from the street above. Some were wearing white robes made of bedsheets; they glinted in the sun. Others had arrived in their street clothes, wearing long-sleeved shirts and thick woolen trousers. The Preacher was leading them in a hymn. They were singing "Gloria in Excelsis Deo," but it sounded in Spitz's ears like a slow dirge rather than a song of praise.

As the hymn ended, the Preacher launched into his speech. "Our Lord Jesus Christ," he intoned, "has told us that to enter the kingdom of heaven we must be born again of water and of the Spirit." He beckoned Clarence and Spitz to join him in the water. Spitz thought how cold the river was, and how swift the current, and he wondered if the congregants would be able to keep their footing. "Here we are washed by the Holy Spirit and made clean," the Preacher said in a clear, crisp voice. "Here we are clothed with Christ."

He led the gathered assembly in another hymn as the Child Prodigy, Rube, and Ray passed around the wooden plates. After the collection was taken, the Prodigy withdrew to the team bus, out of sight of the congregants, to count the take. The Preacher preached for all he was worth. "We praise you, loving Father, for the gift of your son Jesus. He was baptized in the River Jordan where your Spirit came upon him. We ask you to bless this water, that those who are baptized in it may be cleansed in the water of life."

The baptisms proceeded at a steady pace after that, with Clarence escorting men and women into the rush of water and the Preacher and Spitz immersing them. They performed over fifty baptisms that day in the South Saskatchewan River, Clarence announcing the name of the individual who was ready to be saved and the Preacher making the sign of the cross on each person's forehead. "I baptize you in the name of the Father and of the Son and of the Holy Spirit," he intoned, and then, with Spitz's help, the congregant would be dunked backwards and come up gasping for air.

Spitz couldn't help but see it as an experience that came near to drowning, but he also saw how joyful the baptized were at the end of it. All their sins forgiven, they had the weight of the world lifted off their shoulders. Back on shore after the dunking, each of the congregants seemed to be standing a foot taller. Spitz longed for that feeling, longed for the quietude of forgiveness. He would have asked the Preacher to baptize him too, just to have the feeling again, but he'd already been baptized as a child.

When the ceremony was over and the newly baptized had departed back to their homes, Spitz, Ray, Rube, Clarence and the Preacher gathered on the riverbank. The afternoon sun was warm, but they were still shivering after a day in the cold water. Together they celebrated the success of the Preacher's plan. "We musta made fifty dollars at least," Rube crowed.

"Folks like baptisms," the Preacher said. "Where's the Prodigy gotten to?"

"He went back to the bus with the collection," Rube replied.

"Let's find out how much we made."

They trudged up the riverbank, through scrubby Saskatoon berry bushes, to the street above. When they arrived at the bus, they found no sign of the Prodigy or of the money. The collection plates were piled neatly, one atop the other, on the hood of the bus. They searched the dugouts and the area underneath the stands, and then they headed back toward the river. "Anybody see him go into the water?" the Preacher asked.

Nobody had.

"Cuz I don't know if the Prodigy can swim."

They stood on the bank and called his name for the better part of an hour. There was no response. They split up and scoured the bank for a mile in both directions but could find no sign of their absent friend.

The Prodigy had been the Preacher's right-hand man, so nobody was prepared to accuse him of anything. The thought that their teammate might have absconded with the day's earnings, leaving the rest of them high and dry, was unbearable. Spitz tried to banish the thought from his mind, but he could see that Rube and Clarence were thinking it too.

14. The Klan

They combed the city backwards and forwards, up and down and crossways, the next morning, but the Prodigy had disappeared without leaving so much as a thank you note. The Preacher was especially disconsolate. The Child Prodigy had been his pillar to lean on through most of the tour, keeping track of dates and times and riding shotgun, map and compass in hand. Having seen so much hardship and betrayal in the early days of the Depression, the Preacher was at last prepared to entertain the notion that the Prodigy had run off with the baptismal earnings. He steered the bus west out of the city in the early afternoon, looking like a dog with a tin can tied to its tail.

Rosmers was a quaint little town on Highway Number Seven. It featured a rather new brick schoolhouse and an ancient livery stable that had seen better days. There were scores of freshly painted wood frame houses, all looking as though their tenants might be businessmen and lawyers. Across the highway stood a railway station house. The tracks ran in both directions as far as the eye could see across a vast tabletop of prairie. Everything was laid out in straight lines and ninety-degree angles, as if God had somehow created a world based on solid mathematics. The town lots were square, the buildings were square, and the highway skirted the village in a straight line, running parallel to the railway tracks. There were not a lot of trees, but the hedges and picket fences were tidily shaped at right angles.

Spitz was feeling about as happy as an owl in a sleet storm when they arrived. He was blue about his own behavior over the past three days and down and out about the Prodigy's unexplained departure. He wanted to cash in his chips and leave, but he knew that the Preacher had nothing to pay him with. And then there was Ray. Spitz couldn't leave him alone, at the mercy of the road. He owed Ray that much. To top it off, Spitz had gone cold turkey since Saskatoon, not by choice but because liquor was nowhere to be found. He felt washed out and slightly nauseous as he got off the bus.

Situated near the school, the baseball diamond was well-appointed, with a new home run fence and players' benches with backs on them, the kind one might see in a public park in any American city. The five remaining Appalachian All-Stars slumped morosely on the visitors' bench and donned their cleats. Rube had been complaining about his throwing arm for the past three days. When the Preacher asked him how he was feeling, Rube didn't sugar-coat it. "Feels like my wing is about to fall off," he said. "I saw three buzzards circling it in Saskatoon."

The Preacher turned to Spitz. "Sure you can't give us an inning or two?"

"I told you at the start," Spitz said. "I ain't gonna pitch no more."

"People ought to forgive themselves," the Preacher replied. "Cats and dogs do." He turned to Clarence, who was boning his bat near the on-deck circle. "You used to throw some, back in yer Homestead days?"

"I was just a thumber," Clarence protested. "They'd put me in when the game was outta reach."

"Well, yer startin today," the Preacher decreed. "Rube's at first. Spitz is at short. Ray in the outfield. We'll keep 'em on the ground if we can."

Nothing was said between the two coaches before the game began, but there was a strangeness in the way the game was played and viewed. The home team didn't bother to converse with the All-Stars at moments where conversations might usually happen, around first base and in the batter's box. The spectators sat in the bleachers like cardboard cut-outs, never speaking, not even to each other. Spitz thought they were perhaps ardent students of the game, quietly analyzing every move, cigarettes dangling from their lips. They sat and smoked and watched.

Clarence pitched surprisingly well. He didn't have much junk, but he could still throw the ball hard. For a change of pace, he delivered what he called the dead fish, a looping mid-air throw that scraped the heavens and then came crashing down over home plate like a meteorite from the sky. With this arsenal of pitches, he managed to stymie the Rosmers' hitters until the ninth inning.

When the evening sky began to darken, Spitz smelled kerosene and burning wood. At first, he thought a house might be on fire, somewhere in the town. Looking over his shoulder in the direction of the livery barn, he saw a familiar sight. It sickened him to his core. There, beside the barn, was a gargantuan burning cross, its flames leaping skyward against the dusk. Standing motionless near the foot of the cross was a column of men. They were wearing the familiar white robes and pointed hats, the same detestable uniforms Spitz had seen, on occasion, in his home state when he was a boy.

Spitz called time, and he conferred with Clarence and the Preacher at the mound. "Don't like the looks of this," he said.

"Me neither," Clarence replied. "I thought these Canadians was a gentle, polite sort of people."

"I think we oughta git while the gittin's good," Spitz said.

The Preacher put the kibosh on that way of thinking. "We got to finish the goddamn game, or we won't git paid."

Clarence continued to pitch. He struck out the first batter and induced the second batter to hit a weak ground ball. Spitz fielded it and threw the man out by three steps. The column of Klansmen started marching toward the field. Clarence was still working on the third batter when they arrived behind the backstop. They filed on to the diamond and stood, like pale ghosts, ten feet back of the first and third baselines, in foul territory. As Clarence went into his windup, they began to sing "Daddy Stole Our Last Clean Sheet and Joined the Ku Klux Klan," slowly, deliberately. They weren't tuneful. They should stick to burning crosses, Spitz thought; they weren't very good at singing.

The Preacher called time and walked out on to the diamond. "Yer singin is putting me to sleep," he announced. "Please back off and let us finish the game."

They continued to sing as Clarence proceeded to throw. With the count at two-and-two, the batter fouled two pitches off. Reaching back and kicking toward home, Clarence threw the third strike, an embarrassingly slow dead fish that screwed the poor batsman into the ground.

The Preacher made a beeline to the manager of the Rosmers' team and collected his twenty-five dollars. As he was pocketing the cash, he heard a commotion on the field behind him. When he turned to look, he saw Clarence sprinting across the parking lot toward the train station. No one was faster than Clarence. The Klansmen ran awkwardly in pursuit of him, sometimes tripping over the hems of their flowing robes, sometimes over each other. One of them was carrying a length of rope that got tangled between his legs as he ran, causing him to fall head-first onto the gravel.

Soil and sand were spraying off Clarence's cleats, like dirt off a racehorse's hooves, as he put distance between himself and his pursuers. The Preacher saw him disappear behind the station house. "Thanks fer the ball game," he said to the hometown manager. "We'll hafta do it again sometime."

Everyone but Clarence was back on the bus by the time the Preacher got behind the steering wheel. He fired up the infernal machine and headed across the highway toward the station house. In the distance, Clarence was running hard toward a stand of trees. The Klansmen were four hundred yards behind him and losing ground. The Preacher steered the bus back on to the highway and sped along for a quarter of a mile until he found a level crossing. He pulled out into a field of wheat, grain-dust rising behind the bus as he sped through the foot-high crop. Pedal to the floor, he passed the flagging Klansmen and closed the distance between the bus and Clarence. He slowed to ten miles an hour and threw open the door. "Jump on!" he shouted to Clarence. "Let's blow this pop stand!"

Clarence was breathing hard when he leapt onto the bus, caught on the steps by Spitz and Rube. He smiled broadly as they raced across the stunted field of wheat toward another gravel road that would take them away from that hopeless burg.

"You okay?" Spitz asked him.

Clarence smiled even more broadly. "I thought these Canadians were a polite, gentle sort," he said again.

It was pitch-dark by the time they got to Unity, a pretty little town and hopefully friendlier than Rosmers had been. They overnighted by the local school, sleeping on the bus while the few remaining chickens warbled softly on their perches. Spitz was beginning to find the chickens comforting. They reminded him of home.

The next morning, Clarence was busy by the fire, stirring a porridge that had become their staple over the past few days. It was a glutinous concoction, composed of roughly milled oats and water. The best that could be said of it, Spitz thought, was that it stuck to your ribs. And to your teeth. And to your shirt. And to the plate. And to the pot it was cooked in. He didn't dare to complain because complainers were generally given the job they complained about in that outfit, but enough was enough. "Sure would be nice to change things up once in a while," he muttered as he was spooning the gruel into his mouth.

Clarence looked at him archly. "How do you mean?"

"I dunno," Spitz said. "Like maybe bacon and eggs once every week."

"You see any pigs around here?"

Spitz thought it best to pull in his horns. "Don't get me wrong," he said. "I ain't complainin. You're a damn good cook, Clarence."

Clarence wasn't placated. His eyes looked like two piss-holes in a snowbank. "Sounds a little like complainin to me."

Spitz had to think fast. "There's still some birds on the bus," he said. "They're hens, ain't they?"

"Last time I checked."

"How come they ain't layin no eggs?"

"I dunno," Clarence said. "You'll hafta ask them."

An idea came upon Spitz at that moment. He placed his bowl of porridge on a fender and got back on the bus. Finding some battered baseballs in the bottom of the team equipment bag, he set about making nests in cardboard boxes on the back seats of the bus. He found some dead quack grass and leaves and piled them in a heap in each box. Then he placed the baseballs, their leather soft and scarred from too much use, in the middle of each nest. With this ruse, he thought to himself, he would train those hesitant hens to begin laying.

It was full daylight when they saw the local stationmaster walking across the school grounds toward them. He was a lanky old fellow, smoking a pipe and sending up smoke signals that could probably be seen in neighboring towns and villages. He approached the Preacher, who was washing his face in a basin on the steps of the school. "You the baseball players?" the old man asked.

The Preacher wrung his washcloth out in the basin. "You betcha."

"Telegram came fer you yesterday," the stationmaster said. "Mighty strange, if you ask me." He handed the Preacher a sheet of blue telegraph paper.

"Thanks," the Preacher said.

"This is a happy little town," the stationmaster replied. "We don't want no trouble."

"Ain't gonna be no trouble."

"You sure about that?" The old man gave him a hard look, then turned and walked away. The Preacher dried his face with a towel and read the telegram.

When he came back to the bus, the Preacher's eyes were brimming with tears. "They killed the Prodigy," he said in a hoarse whisper.

"Killed the Prodigy?" Spitz replied. "Who?"

"Them fucking gangsters." The Preacher sobbed the words out, tears streaming now.

Ray chimed in. "I knew the Prodigy wouldn't double-cross us."

"The Prodigy was a stand-up guy," Rube added.

"You sure he's dead?" Spitz asked.

"It says here they got him."

The Preacher passed the telegram around for all to see. Spitz read it aloud slowly. "WE GOT YOUR MIDGET STOP WE'RE COMING FOR THE REST OF YOU STOP."

"We shoulda shot that second son-of-a-bitch," the Preacher said, "when we had the chance."

Spitz shook his head. "Killin don't solve nothin," he said. "There's always gonna be bastards in the world."

The Preacher blew his nose into a handkerchief. "Well," he said, "if they're gonna declare war on us, we're gonna declare war on them." He turned to Rube. "You still got your piece, doncha?"

"Yup."

"I'm gonna need you to carry it with you at all times."

"Even on the field of play?"

"Even on the field of play. I'll get the Prodigy's Colt .45 out of the equipment bag. If we see that gangster anywhere, he'll be eatin lead."

They played like men possessed that night, scoring nineteen runs in the first at-bat. Nothing got through the infield in their defensive innings. Clarence lobbed in the dead fish, and the Unity players pounded the ball into the ground. Spitz charged in hard all evening and threw baserunners out with ease. On the one pop fly of the evening, Rube pulled his revolver from a leg holster outside his baseball sock and shot the orb in mid-air. The ball landed in two pieces, half in foul territory and half in fair. Inspecting the masses of leather and string, the umpire ruled the ball dead.

"Dead?" Rube asked.

"Well, look at it," said the ump. "It surely ain't alive."

Rube couldn't argue with that. The batter was called back to the plate for another swing of the bat, and Clarence promptly struck him out with high heat.

The locals, for their part, thought it an uncommon entertainment. Not only did five ex-major leaguers show their prowess with bat and glove, but they also offered a feat of marksmanship with the revolver. The prevailing opinion was that it was the best damn baseball game any one of them had ever seen.

15. Shoot-Out

They arrived in Battleford the next morning to the wheeze of the calliope and the roar of the lion. The circus had come to town a day earlier.

Rube loved circuses as much as he loved baseball and puppies. After breakfast, he wandered down to the fairgrounds by the river. Spitz imagined him petting the grey elephants, their skin wrinkled and dry as parchment. He remained at the fairgrounds for the rest of the day, probably jibing with carnies and clowns. By four in the afternoon, the Preacher began to worry about him. "We best go down there and rescue the happy-go-lucky son-of-a-bitch," he said to Spitz.

"Rescue him from what?"

"From his own stupid self."

The circus was in high gear by the time Spitz and the Preacher arrived. They found a seat in the multi-colored tent, the smell of camel shit pungent in their noses. The first act was a comedic turn, with seven or eight clowns climbing in and out of a motorized vehicle the size of a rocking chair. It was hilarious, Spitz thought, all those painted gentlemen with their red noses and gigantic shoes trying to fit into that small car. One of the clowns was a big fellow with a sad painted-on face. He looked kind of familiar. There was something about his ambling gait, even in those huge shoes he was sporting, that Spitz recognized. It took him a moment or two, but Spitz finally understood that the clown was Rube. Somehow, he'd talked himself into the act.

For a has-been baseball player, Rube was also a pretty good clown. Spitz sat beside the Preacher, and a spirit of heavy sadness descended upon him. He silently reflected on the dual nature of mankind, how there's a personality that we show to the rest of the world and there's another man deep inside that is our own true self. Spitz looked on as Rube attempted the Sisyphean task of squeezing his big body into the little vehicle, and he thought to himself how much closer the clown was to Rube's true nature than the self he commonly presented to the outside world.

When the clown act ended, there was more loud calliope music and then some white horses and some trick riding, a pretty lady standing on a saddle as a horse galloped around the ring. Then came the elephants, standing on their hind legs and dancing while a miniscule trainer shouted directions at them. When the elephants were done, the lions slinked gracefully into the ring. Spitz was close enough to see their eyes, blood-shot and drug-laden. They looked like animal versions of the hobos he had seen in Saint Louis and Des Moines, dulled by years of hardship and servitude, worn down like hoodoos in the sand-blasted desert.

A whip in one hand and a chair in the other, the lion tamer entered the ring. He was dressed in a black tuxedo, three sizes too small for him. Because he was wearing no makeup, Spitz could see instantly that the lion tamer was Rube. He cracked his whip at the big cats. Hesitant at first, they each climbed up on sturdy boxes in the center of the ring. Rube cracked his whip again and shouted a command at the most docile-looking lion, who immediately roared his displeasure, revealing a set of canines that would have sent a herd of zebras bolting across the savannah. Unafraid, Rube dropped the whip and placed the chair on the soft sawdust of the ring. With one hand on the big cat's upper jaw and one hand on the lower, Rube pried the lion's mouth open and inserted his own head between the animal's vice-like mandibles. The audience oohed and awed.

The Preacher turned to Spitz. "Christ!" he said. "Is Rube lookin to git hisself killed?"

After the lions, there were other clown acts and then a camel that slouched around the ring and balanced on his two front legs. The calliope fired up again, this time with climactic grandeur. An emcee announced that, for one time only, there would be an aerial display on the high trapeze with a first-time aerial artiste. "The magnificent men on the flying trapeze," he shouted into a megaphone, "are without fear or any desire for self-preservation." A safety net was strung into place ten feet above the ring. The music blasted again, and the audience was directed to look toward the ceiling in one end of the grand tent where two men in tights were perched atop a steel pole.

One of the trapeze artists was Rube. His partner, a lithe bald fellow, was the first to swing out into the open air. He skipped from one trapeze to another, at last finding his footing on a high pedestal at the other end of the tent. There was a pause, and the music died down. Rube swung out on his own trapeze and made several passes high over the safety net, gaining momentum with each pass. Then his partner swung out, as well, timing his re-entry against Rube's trajectory. Rube let go of his trapeze in mid-swing, executing a crafty airborne somersault. He reached his arms out to be grasped by his partner, but his partner grazed Rube's fingertips and could not grip his hands. Rube went tumbling to the safety net, not with a graceful swan dive but with the awkwardness of a buck-shot goose. A lady screamed just before he hit the edge of the safety net and bounced sprawling into the sawdust.

Rube did not get up immediately. A clown ran out and administered smelling salts. After a moment, Rube sat up and smiled. One of his eyes was looking straight at the crowd. The other, Spitz could see, was gazing off sideways. His left arm was hanging limply at his side.

The Preacher shook his head ruefully. "Looks like Rube won't be fit to pitch tonight either."

Playing that night with four men in the field was not easy. Clarence pitched. The Preacher caught. Spitz played first base, and Ray alternated between left field and shortstop. Rube roamed around the grandstand with his arm in a sling, petting dogs and chatting up the local gals. There was a strong contingent of African Americans in the crowd that night, and they cheered for Clarence with great glee.

Ray had trouble fielding groundballs. They bounced off his kneecaps and elbows, caroming into the outfield while the Battleford team raced around the bases. When he did manage to find the ball in his glove, Ray's throws were so errant that Spitz was pulled twenty feet off first base to catch them.

"What did I tell ya?" the Preacher muttered to Spitz, on the bench, between the sixth and seventh innings. "The ball will find the one guy who shouldn't have it. Every time."

"He's doin his best," Spitz muttered back. "Give the poor guy a chance."

The Appalachians lost by a narrow margin.

After the game, Clarence had a conversation through the backstop screen with a handsome man named Joseph Mayes. Spitz could hear their conversation from the grass nearby, where he was shoving baseball bats into a gunny sack. Mayes told Clarence about the community he was part of, up there near a village named Maidstone, not far away. The Shiloh Colony, as he called it, was a place where Black men and women could homestead the land, free of segregation and disenfranchisement. Mayes' people had come up north in 1909 to escape the racism in Oklahoma.

"Do you play baseball there?" Clarence asked him.

"We play every kind of sport," Mayes said. "We do pretty much as we please." The land, he told Clarence, was verdant, even in these straightened times. They grew oats and wheat, raised cows and chickens, and sold their produce at farmers' markets and in stores. They had just built a Baptist church. "You would be welcome in the community."

Clarence didn't have to think too long about the offer. He went to the Preacher, who was sitting on the players' bench, drinking from a water jug. "This here's my last game," Clarence said.

The desertion was not entirely unexpected, especially after the reception Clarence had been given in Rosmers two days earlier. Still, the Preacher was rankled. "Yer quittin?" he said. "We only have one game left on the tour."

"Yer gonna hafta play it without me."

"Who's gonna pitch fer us now?" the Preacher complained. "Rube's injured. Spitz won't do it. And Ray ain't no pitcher of any kind."

Clarence shrugged. "I'm sure you'll think of somethin."

The Preacher sat with this for a moment, sullen as an ancient goat. "Whatcha gonna do up here anyway?"

"I found my people," Clarence replied. "There's homesteads. And they got a church."

"A Baptist church?"

"Damn right."

"Well, at least they got the right denomination." The Preacher had to smile. "I guess this team's bin fallin apart since the moment we left St. Louis." He held out his hand for Clarence to shake. "Gonna miss you, pard. You were as reliable as they come."

"And you were good to me," Clarence replied. "Fer that I am appreciative."

"Now git outta here," the Preacher said, "before a tear runs down my leg."

Clarence gathered his belongings from the bus, his duffle bag filled with clothes and ointments and baseball gear. He left his uniform folded neatly on the seat. Encountering Spitz as he descended the stairs of the bus one last time, Clarence shook his hand heartily. "Love ya, Spitzy," he said. "I hope you find the peace yer lookin for."

"I hope so too," Spitz said.

"Come see me some time," Clarence added. "I'll have a plot of land and a gallon of good corn whisky."

"I'd like that," Spitz said, trying to be cheerful, but he could not hide his sadness. He watched as Clarence threaded his way into the parking lot, watched as he was surrounded by people who admired him and who shared a common history. Clarence climbed into the back of a flat-bed truck with ten other men and women. He looked at Spitz and waved as the truck pulled out on the gravel road and descended into the river valley and out of sight.

The team, or what there was left of it, camped that night on a flat by the river about a quarter of a mile from a hospital. The Battleford coach had promised it would be a quiet spot. There was a cemetery a few hundred yards away. The Preacher had been looking for a good quiet place where it was possible to get some shut eye.

Not able to will himself to sleep, Spitz meandered down the road to the hospital at dusk. It was an immense brick building with barred-up windows and only a few entrances and exits. A sign over the double doors, at front, read SASKATCHEWAN

MENTAL HOSPITAL. Spitz could hear no sounds from the inmates who were locked away inside. There was no movement on the grounds, no doctors or nurses ferrying patients about.

Spitz made his way to the river. He needed a drink desperately, but he hadn't managed to procure a bottle of anything. The riverbank was laden with perfectly rounded stones, made so by the erosion of the swift current. Spitz picked up a stone and lobbed it into the stream, watching it sink in the cold, deep water. He picked up another stone and examined its grainy texture. It was perfect. He put the stone in his pocket. And another perfect stone and then another. Soon his pockets were full to bulging with perfect stones. Spitz could feel the weight of them, how they worked with gravity, pulling his body toward the center of the earth. He felt a heaviness and a lightness at the same time.

He waded into the swift-running water, up to his waist. His dungarees were soaked, and the thick denim was heavy now too. Spitz gazed into the dark water. In that water, there was no pain and no regret and no memory. It would be another kind of baptism. A new world, a different world, awaited under there. Carried away by its relentless current, Spitz would be forgotten. He waded further in, felt the river tugging at him. What kind of a world was on the other side? When he was a child, Spitz felt like he knew the answer to that question. His life had been a process of forgetting, and now he had no inkling of his own immortality. He waded further in, almost to the point where he lost his footing.

"You vant come along?" a voice behind him said. The accent was thick but indeterminate.

Spitz turned to look at the man. He cut a burly figure even in his institutional garb.

"You vant come vith me?"

"Where?"

"I build a ship. I sail it to zee Hudson Bay. And zen I go back to Iceland." The man smiled at Spitz disarmingly. Even in the twilight, Spitz could see that he had no teeth. Where his teeth should have been, there were instead rusty metal screws that had been inserted somehow in the man's upper and lower jaws.

Trembling in the cold water, Spitz peered at the madman. "Don't wanna go to Iceland," he said.

"You sure?" the man asked through his scrap metal teeth. "Is beautiful."

"I'm sure."

Just then, a nurse came walking briskly to the river's edge. Her spotless white dress glowed in the moonlight. She looked a bit like Joan Crawford, tall and straight and no funny business. "Mister Sukannen," she said, her voice clipped as a new haircut, "it's time for your bath."

The man gave her an unhappy look, like she'd spoiled a day at the beach. All the excitement left his body, and he seemed like a child. "Don't need no bath."

"Nevertheless, it's time," the stern nurse said.

Sukannen winked at Spitz. "I see you here tomorrow night," he whispered. "And zen ve make the journey." With no more prodding than that, he trudged back toward the front doors of the hospital.

The nurse regarded Spitz with a wary eye. "You should come out of the river now."

"Yes, ma'am."

"A lot of people think they have no reason to live," she said. "But if you think about it, there are plenty of reasons." She stood and watched as Spitz trudged back on to the riverbank, and then she marched briskly toward the hospital's front doors.

Heading toward the bus, Spitz saw the headlights of an automobile creeping down the incline into the river valley. At first, he didn't think anything of it. He thought it was a doctor coming for a night shift or a pair of lovers seeking sanctuary from the town. But there was something about the automobile and its behavior that made Spitz suspicious. It stopped at the edge of a clearing, and the headlamps were extinguished.

The night was bright, a full moon nesting in the east, as Spitz emptied his pockets and stepped on to the bus. His dungarees and his tee-shirt were soaked, and he rummaged in his duffle bag for a dry change of clothes. The Preacher was a witness to this act. "Yer soakin wet," he said.

"Yeah, I fell in the river," Spitz told him. "It was an accident." Spitz changed into his dress trousers and a button-down shirt and sat down in a seat across from Ray. He opened a window and listened to the gurgling of the river. Rube must have heard that same gurgling because he brought his big carcass to a standing position and shuffled off the bus. "Gotta piss," he muttered. Spitz could see his dirty white sling until it disappeared in a clump of bushes.

The chickens grumbled from their back seat roosts. Ray was playing "It's Only a Paper Moon" on the harmonica. Listening to that and to the babbling of the Saskatchewan River, the moon so close you could almost touch it, Spitz forgot his worries for a moment. He thought how good life was at its core. He remembered his childhood when the green leaves seemed greener than green somehow, and the sky bluer than blue. He thought of Gwendolyn and the blue of her eyes. He bathed, for a moment, in the purity of her love.

Then he heard the report of a gun.

The Preacher startled awake in his seat at the front of the bus. "What the hell was that?"

"Sounded like gunfire," Spitz said.

"Where's Rube?"

"Went to relieve himself."

"Did he take his gun with him?"

"Dunno."

The Preacher grabbed the Child Prodigy's Colt .45 from the equipment bag and squeezed open the door. "I'd better go take a look."

Ray stopped playing his harmonica. "What's goin on, Spitzy?"

Spitz wanted to comfort him. "Prob'ly just Rube takin a little target practice, that's all."

"Target practice in the dark?"

"Well, you know Rube."

Two more gunshots rang out, and Spitz saw the Preacher sprinting toward the hospital. Another man seemed to be chasing him. He couldn't be sure, in the moonlight, but Spitz thought he recognized the gangster he'd last seen in Minot. There was something about the man's demeanor, and his wide-legged gait, that was identifiable.

"What's goin on?" Ray asked again.

"I ain't sure," Spitz whispered back, thinking how sad it was to be the only man without a gun in a gunfight. "You'd best git down on the floor, okay?"

"On the floor?"

"Yeah."

"Why, Spitzy?"

"You know how Rube is," Spitz said. "Firin off his goddamn pistol in all directions. He might accidentally hit someone."

"He might accidentally hit me?"

"He might."

Ray crouched on the floor of the bus, between two seats, and Spitz covered him with a grey blanket. "You jus' stay right here and don't say a word," Spitz told him. "I'm gonna see what's goin on." There were more gunshots echoing from the vicinity of the hospital. Spitz's blood ran cold.

"I'm ascared, Spitzy," Ray said from under his blanket.

"There ain't nothin to be afraid of," Spitz replied. He found a baseball bat in the equipment bag, a thirty-five-inch piece of hickory, and felt the weight of it in his right hand. In the absence of a gun, a baseball bat would have to do. "I'm gonna go out there and take a look. You jus' stay right there. And don't let nobody on this bus unless it's me or Rube or the Preacher."

From under the thick woolen blanket came Ray's muffled voice. "I won't let nobody on the bus."

Bat in hand, Spitz ventured out on to the grounds. Lights came flickering on from inside the hospital's barred windows, streaming into the dark, threatening to reveal Spitz's movements. Keeping low and silent, he scurried across the flat toward the building.

"Spitzy!" The voice came from behind a squat clump of wolf willow. "Spitzy!" Rube raised his head above the thicket. "It's me, Spitzy. It's Rube."

There was more gunfire from somewhere near the hospital. Spitz took cover with Rube behind the willows. "What's goin on?"

Rube was breathing hard. "The bastards ambushed me, Spitzy. Shot my social finger clean off." Rube held up his hand. In the pale moonlight, Spitz could see the blood and the absence of a finger on Rube's right hand. He dug into his pocket and handed Rube a handkerchief.

"How many gangsters are there?"

"Four, I think. I shot one of 'em and the Preacher plugged another." Rube was busy wrapping the handkerchief around his bloody hand. "That sawed-off prick from Minot chased after the Preacher. I'm keepin an eye out for the other guy."

"Can you still shoot all right?" Spitz asked.

Rube chuckled quietly. "My trigger finger's still intact."

Another gunshot rang out. "I'm gonna go help out the Preacher," Spitz said.

"With nothin but a baseball bat?"

"If I can sneak up," Spitz said, "this piece of hickory is good as anything."

Spitz ran hard toward the hospital and encountered no resistance. There was nothing but silence as he peaked around a corner of the building. Seeing no opposition, Spitz ran the length of the hospital's exterior, stopping at the south end of the building. He held his breath and peered around the southwest corner. He could make out two figures in the dark, the lifeless body of a gangster sprawled on the ground and the Preacher standing over him. The Preacher must have heard Spitz because he wheeled and fired off a round. Spitz felt the displacement of air as the bullet whizzed past his head. "It's me!" he shouted, but the Preacher kept firing until he'd emptied all his chambers. Spitz heard the click of the gun's hammer as the Preacher continued to dry fire his weapon. "Al," Spitz said, "it's me. It's Spitz."

"Spitz?" The Preacher was wide-eyed and vibrating. His skin was pale. He was sweating profusely. Finally realizing that he was out of ammunition, the Preacher dropped his Colt .45 on the ground.

Looking at the Preacher's haggard face, Spitz had an inkling of what it must have been like in the trenches at Meuse-Argonne. "Yeah."

"What are you doin here?" The Preacher's voice was guttural.

"I came to help."

"You should get back on the bus," the Preacher growled. "There's one more out there."

"Maybe you scared him off."

"I say we make a run for it." With no more warning than that, the Preacher bolted past Spitz and disappeared around the back of the building.

Still wielding his bat, Spitz crept around the hospital in the opposite direction, toward the river. From his vantage point by the front steps, he could see people standing in the light behind the barred windows, inmates and nurses all in white. They were watching and pointing, and Spitz followed their gaze. They were pointing at a man in a suit frog-marching another man across the flat toward the river. Spitz squinted his eyes to see better in the darkness. And then he ran.

He ran headlong toward the riverbank. When he got there, he could see a gangster shoving Ray over the uneven ground in front of him. Ray cried out as the small branches of willow whipped his face. His slender body was shuddering. "Move it, retard!" the gangster hissed.

Spitz was paralyzed by Ray's helplessness and the gangster's gun. Setting his bat gently on the ground so as not to be heard, Spitz reached down and picked up a stone from the river's edge. He felt the stone in his hand, round and grainy, slightly smaller than a baseball but about the same weight. The gangster kicked the feet out from under Ray and stood above him, pistol pointed at the back of Ray's head. Spitz was about sixty feet away but off to the side, where the gangster couldn't see him. He took a breath, reared and kicked, launching the stone for all he was worth.

A pitcher always knows, as soon as the ball leaves his hand, whether he's thrown a strike or a ball, and Spitz knew full well. He watched the trajectory of the stone as it arced toward the gangster's temple. All his life seemed to be tied up in the flight of that stone, all his remorse over things said and done. Time stood still. For one brief moment, the river stopped flowing. The gangster cocked his gun and gritted his teeth. Ray's body shook. And then the stone connected, pure and simple and round as life and death, crashing into the gangster's temple with the force of a meteorite. Almost in slow motion, the gangster dropped, as Ray had dropped three years before, clutching at the air as if to find some purchase there to keep him from falling, like a cow that had received a bolt to the brain. The gun did not go off.

His feet scraping and sliding across the stony river's edge, Spitz sprinted toward the fallen gangster. There was no life left in the man by the time Spitz arrived. He was not breathing. The dent in the side of his skull was three inches deep. Spitz gently extricated the gun from the gangster's hand.

Ray was squirming to get out from underneath the man's dead carcass. "Git him offa me, Spitzy!"

Spitz rolled the gangster on his side and helped Ray to his feet. "You all right?"

"I'm sorry I opened the door on the bus," Ray said. "I thought he was Rube."

By the time they straggled up from the riverbank, the place was crawling with Mounties, their tunics blazing even in that darkness. Some of them were combing the bushes, looking for fatalities. Others were interviewing doctors and nurses on the front steps of the hospital. Rube was sitting on the steps of the bus, staring at his missing finger and willing it to grow back. Up near a clump of trees where the first two gangsters had been slain, the Preacher was explaining the incident to a burly Mountie who looked like he was about six months from retirement.

The Preacher's face was still pale and clammy, and his hands hadn't stopped shaking. "They kidnapped one of our own," he told the man in scarlet, "and then they came after us."

"How'd these gangsters get here?" the Mountie asked.

"That's their car up on the rise," the Preacher replied, pointing with an unsteady finger. "They abandoned it up there. Took the long walk down to git the drop on us."

"And what time did that occur?"

"Can't be too sure," the Preacher said.

Spitz fished in his own pocket for the watch Gwendolyn had given him. He clicked open the cover. It had stopped at exactly 12.45.

"Let's go take a look at the car," the Mountie said.

Spitz joined the Preacher and the Mountie and together they walked up the long gravel road toward the gangsters' car. It was the same sedan that had stopped for them outside St. Louis, still gleaming and black as a hearse. They approached the vehicle with caution, not knowing if another gangster had been left to guard the getaway car. The Mountie drew his revolver and pulled open the passenger's side door. A machine gun was resting on the seat. There was a sawed-off shotgun on the floor below the glove compartment. The Mountie shook his head. "Looks like they came carrying a grudge."

"They're bastards plain and simple," the Preacher replied. "They already killed one of our boys."

The Mountie squinted at him suspiciously. "Why would they do a thing like that?"

"Ever hear of Fast Eddie Kramer?" the Preacher asked.

"Who?"

"They wanted him to throw the Series a few years back."

"What's he got to do with anything?"

"Eddie was travellin with us, and these guys wanted to do him in."

Just then there was a hollow thumping that sounded, at first, like the wings of a startled prairie chicken. The thumping got louder, and then there was the clanking of metal on metal. It was coming from inside the car. With his gun at the ready, the Mountie edged around the back of the vehicle. He kicked the lock off the trunk. Standing at arm's length, with his handgun cocked and pointed, he slowly lifted the lid of the trunk.

The first thing that appeared, in the pale moonlight, was a tire iron in the shape of a cross. Then the Child Prodigy's misshapen pate rose out of the darkness of the trunk. He looked gaunt and dusty, but he was able to find his voice. "It's about time," he said.

16. Jelly Roll

They stitched up Rube's hand at the hospital, and then the Appalachian All-Stars spent the night in the Battleford jail. To be truthful, Spitz had a better rest that night than he'd had for most of the tour. The cot in the cell was hard and poky, but at least he wasn't having to sleep sitting up. Rube roamed the jail cell in a perpetual circle. The Preacher sat stone-faced and inconsolable. The Child Prodigy droned on and on about his adventures after the kidnapping, and Ray played the harmonica to drive away the blues. After a while, he sang "You're in the Jailhouse Now," his voice high and clear as an angel.

Down the hallway, in the detachment office, a Mountie was talking on the telephone to various agencies in the United States. Spitz could hear the Mountie's dry voice in conversations with the Sherriff's Office in Minot and then with a branch of the FBI. The words "Al Capone" and "rum runners," spoken quietly and seriously, reverberated down the hallway. Spitz only heard one side of the phone calls. The Mountie's voice was soothing in its monotone and, before long, Spitz was fast asleep.

Hustled down to the courthouse the next morning, the five remaining members of the Appalachian All-Stars stood before a grey-bearded, soft-spoken judge. "People died last night," the judge said, after a brief proceeding. "According to the agreed-upon statement of facts, they died at your hands."

The Preacher stood up and addressed the court. "It was them or us, Your Honor."

"That remains to be seen," the judge said, scrutinizing the sad faces before him. "I have no choice but to remand you in custody until such time as your guilt or innocence can be determined."

"But Your Honor," the Preacher protested, "we're expected to play a game of hardball in Prince Albert five days from now."

"That's none of my affair." The judge rapped on his desk with a gavel, and the All-Stars were promptly ushered out of the building and back to the jail.

Spitz was in a funk for the next two days. He wandered around the jail cell, wishing for a drink. His mouth was dry as tinder, and his gullet was parched all the way down to his belly. On the second day, his hands started to shake like the Preacher's hands did, back in Moose Jaw. Spitz covered for himself by keeping his hands in his pockets or by sitting on them whenever he was sitting down. The Preacher noticed, though, and asked him what was wrong.

"Nothin," Spitz said. "I just git a little antsy bein cooped up like this."

"We're all antsy," said the Preacher. "Don't make it any worse by putting the rest of us on edge."

But Spitz could not stop pacing. When it became evident that Spitz couldn't control himself, the Preacher called on Ray to play a tune. "What do you want me to play?" Ray asked.

"Somethin soft and soothing."

Ray played "Amazing Grace" seven times in a row, and it had a calming effect on Spitz. He remembered an old Baptist church back in Dillard, and he remembered Gwendolyn sitting there, dressed all in white, a bonnet covering her pretty blonde hair. He remembered his own ornery father sitting there, singing too. About the only place his dad wasn't ornery was in that church.

It was getting toward suppertime when the burly Mountie came walking back into the cell area. The food prisoners were given to eat was nothing to write home about, but Spitz was still disappointed to see that the Mountie was not proffering plates and bowls. The Mountie stopped in front of the cell and considered how to break his news. "Something terrible has happened," he said. "There's no kind way to put this. I'm afraid Fast Eddie Kramer is dead."

The Preacher stood up. "Fast Eddie?"

"I'm afraid so."

"I told him it was fool-hardy to go back."

"What happened to him?" Spitz asked.

"He was gunned down outside a bar in Chicago," the Mountie replied.

All the blood drained from the Preacher's face. He fell back down on his cot.

"Are you sure?" Spitz asked the Mountie.

"We checked with Chicago P.D. and with the FBI."

"Was it the gangsters who shot him?"

"It appears that was the case."

"Poor Eddie," Ray said.

The cop looked them over. Utter sadness was in his face. "I'm sorry," he said, and then he trudged back into the office.

Maintaining his silence, the Preacher sat staring at the cinderblock walls for over an hour. Ray sat on the cot beside the Preacher and put an arm around him. After some time, the Preacher spoke again. "I warned him not to go back."

"Yes, you did," Spitz said. "You surely did." Spitz had never seen him quite this low before.

"It's dog eat dog out there," the Preacher murmured, his eyes red and hopeless. "Seems like there's them that eats and them that gets eaten."

They were ushered back into court on the third day. The same grey-bearded judge was presiding. He asked the All-Stars to stand, and then he proceeded with his ruling. "Your story checks out," he said, "and we have the gangland slaying of Edward Kramer as proof of that. I can see no evidence to suggest that this was anything other than a matter of self-defense."

The All-Stars breathed a collective sigh of relief that was audible to everyone who was in the courtroom.

"There is another matter that concerns me." The judge peered at them over his wire-rimmed spectacles. "It seems that you have entered this country illegally."

The Child Prodigy spoke up. "We came through at North Portal, yer Honor," he said. "Just like everybody else."

"It seems," the judge continued, "that there is no paperwork to attest to your legal entry."

"Surely then the paperwork must have gotten lost," the Prodigy said.

The judge ruminated on this idea for a moment. "I suppose that's possible. We'd have to wait for further clarification from the border."

"Your Honor," the Preacher said, "we're supposed to play our last game in Prince Albert two days from now."

"So I've been told."

"Then we're headin back south, and we'll be outta yer hair."

"You're going to be needed back here in any case," the judge replied, "and I'm going to need some surety of that. We found ninety-seven dollars and thirty-four cents in the glove box of the gangsters' automobile. I take it that money belongs to you?"

"That's the baptismal collection," the Prodigy fairly yelled. "The gangsters stole it from me."

The judge looked at the All-Stars and cogitated. "I think you are good people," he said at last, "and I'm willing to put my trust in you. I'm hereby releasing you on your own recognizance. But I will need you to appear before me again in ten days' time. The cash from the glovebox will remain with this court as surety." He rapped on his desk with the gavel.

"But we need that money in order to pay our players!" the Prodigy protested.

The judge's feathers were ruffled, and he peered over his glasses at the Prodigy with undisguised rancor in his face.

Stepping in front of the Prodigy, the Preacher said, "That's fair and equitable, your Honor. We will happily abide by your ruling."

When they were back on the bus, Spitz checked the hens and his makeshift nests. The six hens were dutifully warming the baseballs with their nether parts. They grumbled to one another like elderly matrons, heads bobbing with the seriousness of their gossip. They each trilled out a protest when Spitz gently lifted them off the nests to see if his ruse of the baseballs had produced anything edible. No eggs had been laid.

It was a bit of a reunion all the way to Prince Albert. The Prodigy regaled his teammates with stories about how he'd fought off one of the gangsters with a rabbit punch to the crotch and how the others finally managed to hold him down. He would have been killed right there and then, he said, but the gangsters decided that he was worth more alive than dead.

Spitz asked Rube how his hand was.

"Still feelin the pain," Rube said, "but I think my side-hill tweezler will be more effective without that finger."

They arrived in Prince Albert with a day-and-a-half to spare. On the edge of a great pine and deciduous forest, the city was a brawling conglomeration of pulp mills and prisons, of hucksters and businessmen. It had the look of once being a gold rush city and of having fallen on sadder days. The circus they had seen in Battleford a few days earlier had now moved on to Prince Albert. Carnies were setting up their tents down by the river. Their presence improved Rube's morale considerably. In the mid-afternoon, Spitz left Ray in the care of the Preacher and the Prodigy and headed down to a hotel called the National. He drank his fill of hard whisky and beer.

There was a fellow sitting at the other end of the curved wooden bar, watching Spitz as he drank. A tall, slender, good-looking man, he wore buckskin, brain-tanned and beaded in the finest style. Long, thin braids of hair hung down his back. Spitz could smell the pungent odor of the buckskin from ten feet away. It smelled of the forest, open water, and smoke. "You look like you're drinking with a purpose in mind," the man said. He was well-spoken.

"Dunno what business that is of yours," Spitz replied, shooting him a dirty look.

The man held his hands in the air in a gesture of harmlessness. "I was only making conversation."

"There's no need," Spitz said. "I'm happy bein quiet."

"All right."

They sat ten feet apart all afternoon, both men drinking alone and drinking too much. A sickly-looking barman poured them whisky after whisky until Spitz ran out of money. He was getting ready to leave when the barman poured him another drink.

"What's this?" Spitz said. "I'm broke."

"Fella over there bought it fer ya."

Spitz sat down again. "Oh. Okay." He turned to the man in buckskins. "Thanks."

"My pleasure."

Spitz began to regret his ill humor at first meeting the man. "Sorry," he said. "I bin havin a bad couple of years."

The man pushed his own drink down the gnarled bar and sat on a bar stool closer to Spitz. "I think you and I are kindred spirits," he said.

Spitz chuckled. "Well, we both like the same kind of hooch."

The buckskin man placed a green aspen leaf on the bar between them.

"What's that all about?" Spitz asked.

"It's a talisman," the man said. "I carry it with me."

"What's it mean?"

"It means I'm close to nature," the buckskin man continued. "I live by a lake some miles north of here. There's no depression where I live."

"Sounds jiggedy-boo," Spitz said. He took another drink.

The man regarded him cooly. Despite drinking glass for glass with Spitz all afternoon, he did not seem nearly as drunk as Spitz. "You strike me as someone who can't forgive himself."

Spitz thought of a hundred things he could say. He thought of telling the buckskin man to mind his own business again, but there was something disarming in the man's candor. "I feel like an impostor," Spitz admitted.

"We're all impostors," the buckskin man said, "out here in the big, bad world."

They talked it out for hours like that, telling truths and long-held secrets, drinking shots and glasses of beer. By the time the bar closed, at midnight, Spitz was royally drunk. The buckskin man argued with the barkeep over the bill, and then he helped Spitz out to the parking lot where a jalopy awaited.

They didn't go back to the team bus. Instead, they headed north down a narrow gravel road encroached upon by stately evergreens. They crept along at a slow pace. Spitz could see the cycs of brown bears and lynx, staring out at them from the forest, glinting in the beam of the jalopy's one headlight. It was a wild place, this forest, and yet Spitz was unafraid.

At last, the thick wall of forest fell away to reveal a body of water. Deserting their jalopy on the shoreline, the two men climbed gingerly into an awaiting canoe, Spitz hunkered down low in the bow, the buckskin man in the stern. Spitz had never ridden in a canoe before. "Paddle," the man told him, "but stay low." Spitz knelt on the floor of the canoe and felt the cold, black water on his knuckles as he paddled. For what seemed like hours in the moonlight, they paddled. Spitz could not see the shoreline or the crests of trees. He had no idea of the direction in which they were heading, but he felt in his soul that he had to go there.

They disembarked the canoe sometime later and trudged through the forest to a log cabin at the edge of another lake. The buckskin man threw open the door. "Welcome to Ajawaan."

The sun had not yet appeared on the eastern horizon. The buckskin man lit a kerosene lamp, and Spitz looked around the place. There was a makeshift hole in the floor of the cabin. Spitz could see water and a wooden ramp leading up to the hole. The cabin must have been built right over the water. "That's for the beaver," the man told him. "You sleep over there." He pointed with his lips to a long wooden bench at the far side of the cabin.

They had both been asleep for some time when Spitz was awakened by a splashing of water and a scraping of claws along the wet wooden ramp. He opened his eyes to see a huge beaver crawling out of the water toward him. The beaver was massive, the size of a coffee table. It had dark, dark eyes. It stared intently at Spitz for some time, and then it spoke. "All will be forgiven," it said in an old man's voice.

Spitz closed his eyes and opened them again, thinking that he was experiencing the effects of delirium. The beaver was no longer there. Standing before him was the old man, dressed all in white. He was smoking a pipe. Spitz could almost smell the fragrant tobacco. The old man looked at him with cold, dead eyes. "Bring my son home," he said in a clear voice, "and all will be forgiven."

17. The Ball Game

Spitz awoke late the next morning to the flavorful aroma of moose meat and bannock, cooked over a wood-burning stove. The daylight was blinding, even inside the cabin. Sitting up on the hard wooden bench, Spitz rubbed the crusty sleep out of his eyes. The buckskin man was standing over a cast-iron stove, tending to the sputtering frying pan. He regarded Spitz wryly. "Good morning."

"What day is it?" Spitz asked.

"Beats me," the man replied. "Time up here is told by the weather."

"I got to get back to Prince Albert for a ball game."

"A ball game?"

"Yeah."

"What kind of a ball game?"

"A baseball game."

"Only ball game I know is cricket," the man said. "What's baseball like?"

"Kinda like life," Spitz said. "Seven times out of ten, you fail."

"Sounds frustrating."

"It's a learning experience."

"Don't worry," the man said. "I'll get you there on time."

When the two of them were at the table, dining together, Spitz ate voraciously. It was the best meal he'd had since the tour began. The moose meat was hardy and succulent, and the bannock went good with a jar of saskatoon berry preserve that was on the table.

After their breakfast, the buckskin man cleared the table and sat down with a notepad and a pencil. He was immediately distant, absorbed in whatever he was writing. Spitz washed the dishes in a pan filled with cold lake water. "What are you workin on?" Spitz asked.

"Just some random thoughts."

"I thought I saw a fat beaver in the cabin last night," Spitz said. "He came up outta that hole."

"That would be Jelly Roll," the man told him. "He's the corpulent one."

"You live with the beavers?"

The buckskin man placed his pencil gently on the rough wooden table. "I used to trap those intelligent animals and sell their skins for money," he said. "This is my way of rectifying a former wrong."

"I see."

"Do you?" the man asked. "If I can forgive myself for shamelessly killing these beautiful creatures, you can surely forgive yourself for whatever you've done."

"There's some things a man can't forgive himself for." Spitz was scrubbing away at a plate until the enamel was worn almost clean through.

"Every human being, if they live long enough, has regrets in life," the buckskin man replied. "Things they should have done. Things they shouldn't have done. The mark of a person is how they deal with those regrets and what they do to atone."

Spitz considered the man's words for a moment. "I s'pose you might be right."

"I am right," the man said. "You just have to use your God-given talents."

The buckskin man was as good as his word. He returned Spitz to the baseball diamond in Prince Albert by suppertime, and he remained at the ballpark to watch the game. The Preacher greeted Spitz in the parking lot. "Thought you'd deserted me too," he said. "Glad you saw fit to come back."

As they walked to the visitors' bench, Spitz noticed Satchel Paige, in a Prince Albert uniform, warming up on the sidelines. His delivery was unmistakable. There was the slower-than-slow windmill windup, the tall stretch with both arms over his head, the straight-legged kick, toes flexed toward the heavens, and then the delivery, straight over the top, the body like a catapult, the ball heaved with the force of a granite cannonball through the fortified walls of a gated city. The echo of the baseball hitting the catcher's mitt could be heard for miles.

"What the hell's he doin here?" Spitz asked the Preacher.

"They musta paid him the big bucks to come this far north," the Preacher said. He proceeded to run through the day's lineup. Rube's finger still wasn't healed, so he'd have to sit on the bench. The Preacher would try his hand at pitching. The Prodigy would catch. Spitz would play all the infield positions, and Ray would roam the outfield.

Spitz looked back at the buckskin man who smiled and nodded his head. "Fuck it," Spitz said to the Preacher as he was lacing on his cleats. "Give me the ball today."

The Preacher looked at him incredulously. "You?" he said. "D'you mean you wanna pitch?"

"Just give me the fuckin ball."

Before the game started, Paige strolled over to pay his respects to Spitz and the All-Stars. "Spitzy," he said, nodding under his long-billed cap. "Told you I'd come and whoop yer ass one day."

Before Spitz could formulate a reply, the Preacher cut in. "We'll have to see about that."

Paige flashed a smile. "Where's the rest of yer guys?"

"We're so confident in Spitzy here," the Preacher said, "that we decided to field only the four of us."

"The four of ya?"

"Yup."

Paige thought about that for a moment. "Well, if you're playin with four, we're playin with four too."

"Fine by us," the Preacher said.

"Then let's play ball." Paige strode out on to the diamond and called his coach over. There was a brief meeting, and then five of his own players went and sat on the bench. He threw a few warmup pitches, lazy fastballs that looked quite hittable.

The Prodigy stepped up to the plate, crouching low to make his miniscule strike zone even smaller. Paige circled the mound, massaging the ball with his long fingers and chuckling to himself. Stepping on the rubber, he wound up and delivered a fastball low and hard, a copper bee bee knee-high across the plate.

The umpire called a strike. Paige's second pitch was similar, only thrown at greater velocity. The Prodigy didn't offer at it. A second strike was called. The Prodigy crouched even lower. The third strike went by him with a trail of smoke.

"This guy is good," the Preacher said to Spitz, near the on-deck circle.

"Oh yeah."

Next at bat was the Preacher. He flailed at a nine-to-five curve ball and then whiffed on two fastballs up-and-in. He walked back to the bench with his tail between his legs, mumbling some swear words at himself.

Spitz was the next victim. Paige nodded at him as he dug into the batter's box, and then he threw some chin music an inch-and-a-half from Spitz's front teeth. Spitz dropped to the dirt, the bat falling in one direction, his hat fluttering away in another. After Spitz had gotten up and dusted himself off and found his hat and his bat, Paige was standing on the mound, smiling at him. "Don't be digging in on me, Spitzy," he warned.

"Fair enough," Spitz hollered back.

Paige threw two curve balls for strikes and then a fastball, low on the outside corner. Spitz had been looking curve ball all the way, and he popped up a lazy flyball to the center fielder. The top half of the first inning was over.

Spitz collected his glove from the bench and walked tentatively out to the mound. It felt like a foreign territory Spitz had visited in another lifetime. He threw a few warmup pitches. His arm was loose and rubbery. He liked the height of the mound and the downward trajectory of the ball toward the plate. He remembered the confrontation and the dance, pitcher leading, batter following, and umpire calling. He touched up the rosin bag and squinted in as the Preacher flashed a signal from behind the plate. There was a moment of uncertainty before the windup started, as if he couldn't quite remember how, but then Spitz stretched both arms above his head and a recollection washed over him. He balanced like a stork on his right leg, then uncoiled and delivered the ball up-and-in. The hayseed umpire touched the Preacher on the shoulder. "I didn't see the ball," he said, loud enough for Spitz to hear, "but I saw where you caught it."

"Just call strike," the Preacher growled. "This guy don't throw no balls."

"Stee-rike!"

Firing nothing but fastballs, Spitz mowed the first three batters down in order. Paige was standing in the on-deck circle when the inning finished. "That's some pretty sweet work!" he shouted at Spitz. "Now I see what people were talkin about."

In the top of the second inning, Paige did some sweet work himself. He struck Ray out on three pitches. When the Child Prodigy bunted craftily down the third baseline, Paige loped over, gathered up the ball, and threw him out with ease. The Preacher couldn't get around on the inside fastball, as Paige knew, so that was the only kind of ball he saw. On the fourth pitch of the at bat, he popped up weakly to the catcher.

It was Spitz's turn on the mound again, this time facing Paige. Normal baseball protocol would have required that Spitz throw the ball at Paige's ear, but Spitz did not want to hurt anybody. He shook off the Preacher's signal and put a fastball on the outer half of the plate. He had thought Paige was weak in the batter's box, a one-dimensional player, and he was surprised when Paige hit a frozen rope to the center field wall. By the time Ray had gotten the ball in to the Prodigy, Paige was strutting off second base like a prize turkey. Fortunately, the next three batters were not as good. Spitz struck out the rest of the side on nine pitches, leaving Paige stranded.

At the top of the next inning, the Preacher decided it was time to toy with Satchel Paige's legendary confidence. Standing along the third base line, he started razzing Paige in a low voice. "Hey, Satch," he said. "Satch."

Paige didn't pay him no heed. He threw a filthy slider to Spitz, and Spitz almost came out of his cleats swinging at it.

"Hey, Satch," the Preacher reiterated, "we took a vote to decide who was the best-looking player on your team." Paige was a good-looking man and proud of it. He glanced over at the Preacher. "Satch," the Preacher said, "you came in second."

Paige threw another pitch, a rising fastball at the top of the strike zone. Spitz watched it, and the umpire called "Strike!"

"Hey Satch," the Preacher said, just as Paige was letting go of the third pitch, "the rest of the team tied for first."

Whether Paige was thrown off by the remark was debatable, but he delivered an uncharacteristic pitch down the middle, and Spitz clouted it into right field. "Don't be talkin to me no more, old man," Paige hissed at the Preacher as Ray settled into the batter's box. "We might be up here in the bush, but we don't have to play bush league rules."

Ray never lifted the bat off his shoulder in the next at bat. "That guy throws like Dizzy Dean," he said when he got back to the bench.

"How would you know what Dizzy Dean throws like?" the Preacher asked him.

"I think I musta played against him once," Ray said. He looked at Rube. "Didn't I?"

"You surely did," Rube said.

Meanwhile, the Prodigy had decided that waiting for a base-on-balls was not going to work. He swung his child-sized bat with controlled fury but came up empty on every pitch.

Spitz was more wary of Paige in the bottom of the third. He pitched the tall man carefully on the corners, working the count to three-and-two and then putting him away with the fade-away that Carl Mays had taught him. The next two batters were easy work, and Spitz walked back to the bench with a clean inning on the scorecard.

In the fourth inning, Paige seemed to find his stride. He sawed off the Preacher with the first pitch, breaking his bat in two as the ball squibbed up the first base line like an errant snooker shot. The Preacher was irate, not because he'd been put out but because his bat had been broken. "You've no call to do that," he shouted at Paige. "You know I can't afford another bat."

Paige wasn't flustered. "Best you don't swing at that pitch then."

The Preacher walked back to the bench like John McGraw after a fist fight with an umpire.

Equally careful with Spitz as Spitz had been with him, Paige painted corners with his fastballs. Spitz pounded a low outside pitch into the dirt, and it was fielded easily.

Ray went out after that.

"Wish we didn't have to bat him today," the Preacher muttered to Spitz. "He's a sure out."

"If he don't play, I don't play," Spitz said for the umpteenth time.

"Well, it's yer funeral," the Preacher said. He was still bitter over his broken bat. "And mine too, I suppose."

Spitz found some trouble in his half of the fourth. He struck out the first batter, but then Paige rapped a single which Ray fielded cleanly on one hop. The next batter got to first base on an error. As he was about to pitch again, Spitz noticed the buckskin man standing near the backstop. "Use your talents," the man said in clear, low voice.

Spitz struck the next guy out and then the next.

There were only about a hundred people watching the game. The Preacher had said as much a little earlier, when he was mentally calculating the take. As each inning passed, the crowd grew more and more silent, as if cheering might disrupt the perfect balance of the game, the perfect balance of life itself.

In the fifth inning, the Preacher borrowed one of Rube's bats. He knew what to expect. Paige had been throwing him up-and-in all evening, figuring that the Preacher was too old and worn out to get around on his fastball. With two strikes on him, the Preacher opened his stance and stepped in the bucket as he swung. The bat connected, and the Preacher stood at home plate and watched the ball disappear over the left field wall. As he was rounding the bases, the Preacher hollered at Paige, "Hey Satch, if you can find that ball, I'll sign it for you as a memento."

Paige dismissed him with a wave of the hand. "Lucky hit," he shouted back. "Even a blind squirrel finds a nut some of the time."

Spitz started to fade in the sixth. His fastball wasn't hopping anymore. His fadeaway wasn't dropping out of sight like marbles off a table. He was running on fumes, and everybody knew it. Paige waited him out and then swung on a slider that didn't slide. By the time Ray returned the ball to the infield, Paige was standing on third.

The Prodigy was stationed between first and second, so Paige had free rein on the other side of the infield. He danced and skittered down the line, halfway to the plate, as Spitz wound up to pitch. He clapped his hands and whistled. Then, on the second pitch, he broke, speeding toward home. Spitz stepped off the rubber and fired the ball at the Preacher, who was blocking the base. Paige and the ball arrived at the same time. He lowered his shoulder, and there was an explosion of bodies and hats and gloves and balls and catcher's masks. The Preacher landed in the sand behind the batter's box, and the ball dropped out of his glove. Paige was sprawled on top of the plate. The umpire called "Safe!"

The Preacher sat there in the sand for a moment, trying to see straight. When his vision had recovered, he jumped up and punched Paige square in the face. Paige punched him back with a jolt that must have caused the Preacher's ears to ring, and then the umpire stepped in between them. "If you two aren't gonna play ball," he said, "I'm gonna call this game here and now."

Dabbing some blood from his earlobe, the Preacher turned to the ump and growled, "We'll play until this is over." Paige gave the Preacher a polite shove and walked past him to the bench.

In the seventh inning, Paige made changes on the mound. His windup grew more compact. He varied the height of his leg kick to throw the batters' timing off. He stopped throwing fastballs altogether, choosing instead to inundate hitters with curves and fadeaways and even the odd changeup. In the eighth, he walked Spitz on four pitches, keeping him at first while he struck out the rest of the side. The Preacher razzed Paige something terrible for that. "Hey Satch," he shouted, "are you afraid to pitch to our boy over there?"

"I ain't afraid to pitch to you," Paige shouted back.

The game was tied at one run apiece in the bottom of the ninth when Spitz took the mound. Calling time as the first batter was readying himself, the Preacher ambled on to the field and conferred with Spitz. "How you feelin?"

"I'm throwin nothin but pus," Spitz said.

"Think you can suck it up fer one more inning?"

"I think so."

"Do that," the Preacher said, "and we'll score you a run in the tenth."

They struck out the first batter on slow curve balls. The second batter popped up behind second base, and the Prodigy raced across the diamond, laid out, and caught the ball a foot off the ground. Then Paige stepped into the batter's box.

Spitz had nothing left, and Paige knew it. When Spitz threw a first pitch fastball on the outside corner, Paige rifled it down the first base line. Spitz thought the game was over, but the ball faded into foul territory moments before it left the field. As he returned to the batter's box, Paige flashed Spitz a smile. "Almost gotcha that time," he said. Spitz threw him another fastball, high, out of the strike zone, and Paige fouled it into the stands. Then he threw him three curve balls, hoping Paige would chase, but with no luck.

The count stood at three and two when the Preacher called time again. He walked out to the mound and put his arm around Spitz's aching shoulder. "Why'nt you throw him the old spitter?"

"I ain't got control over that pitch."

"I think you should throw it nevertheless."

Spitz shook his head. "We'll get him with the curve ball."

"Okay then," the Preacher said.

When the Preacher was set up again behind the plate, Spitz didn't bother to look in for a sign. He rocked back and kicked and threw the curve ball as hard as he could. He watched as the ball arced toward the inside corner, watched as Paige shifted his weight and brought his hands inside the ball. The bat connected with an unmistakable thwack, and Spitz ducked involuntarily as the ball streaked past him toward centerfield. He turned and saw Ray standing there, fortuitously in line with Paige's drive. Ray lifted his glove at the last possible moment. The ball, hit hard and fading, glanced off Ray's weathered mitt and went bounding toward the outfield fence. Ray looked in his glove. Not sure where the ball had gone, he called to the infield for advice. The Prodigy pointed toward the fence in right center, and Ray sprinted in that direction. Paige scampered around the bases. By the time Ray had found the ball and thrown it to the Prodigy, Paige had already crossed home plate.

The Prince Albert bench erupted with hugs and cheers and fist pumps. They hoisted Paige on their shoulders and paraded him up and down the first base line. The crowd of onlookers was as loud as a hundred people could be. Spitz and the Preacher watched their celebration. "You deserved the win," the Preacher whispered to Spitz.

"No." Spitz shook his head. "Paige deserved it."

"I told you before," the Preacher replied. "The ball has a way of finding the guy who shouldn't have it."

Spitz was too tired to argue, and the Preacher was still bleeding from his ear.

Then Paige came over and shook Spitz's hand. "You were even better than I thought."

"And you were as advertised," Spitz said.

On the bench after the game, as they were taking off their cleats, Ray started weeping. They were soft tears at first, but then he was sobbing. "I'm sorry, Spitzy," he said. "I'm so sorry."

Spitz put his arm around Ray. "Don't be sorry," he replied. "That ball was hit hard."

"I shoulda caught it, Spitzy."

"No one coulda caught that thing," Spitz said.

Ray looked happier after that. He wiped his nose on his sleeve and smiled.

Later, on the bus, Rube punched Spitz playfully on the shoulder with his good hand. "Looks like you found yer way back," he said.

Spitz nodded.

"And it's about time too," said the Preacher.

Spitz tossed his glove on the seat and proceeded to the back of the bus. The hens were dutifully warming baseballs, clucking disdainfully in the backs of their throats. Gently lifting one of them, Spitz saw three warm, brown eggs among the baseballs in the nest. "Looks like we're havin omelets for breakfast tomorrow."

Early the next morning, the Preacher and Spitz were sitting on a curbstone in the parking lot, sopping up egg yolks with pieces of bread. Rube stepped off the bus, hoisting a duffle bag over his broad shoulder. "Where are you off to?" the Preacher asked.

"Think I found my true calling," Rube said. "I'm runnin away with the circus."

A calliope sputtered and chimed in the distance.

The Preacher looked at him like he was crazier than a shithouse rat. "You sure you wanna be doin that?"

"Ain't got nothin better to do," Rube replied, "now that baseball season's over."

"Well, God bless you then."

18. The Way Home

It was a big bus for just four people, but Spitz and Ray and the Preacher and the Prodigy had a grand time of it. They didn't bother returning to Battleford for their ninety-seven dollars and thirty-four cents. Happy with the money they'd earned in Prince Albert, they made a beeline for the international boundary, crossing the border at night on a side-road when nobody was watching. They ate omelets the next morning just outside of Kenmare and arrived in Minot by three in the afternoon. Spitz and Ray took their leave in that fair city.

The Preacher gave them each twenty dollars cash and shook their hands. "You stuck it out to the bitter end," he said to Spitz. "And loyalty is something I truly prize."

"I wouldn't leave ya hangin," Spitz said.

"I know. I know you wouldn't." The Preacher wiped something out of his left eye. "Goddamn dust is everywhere," he said. "Listen. I might be startin her up again next year. If ya wanna tag along."

"Let's talk about it when the time comes."

"Okay."

"What are you gonna do with the rest of them chickens?" Spitz asked.

"Figger I'll drop them off back in Johnsonville."

"That's a good idea."

The Prodigy shook Spitz's hand. "Take good care of Ray," he said. Ray was standing on the curb with his duffle at his feet.

"I will. And you take care of the old preacher man here."

"You know it."

The Preacher and the Prodigy stepped back onto the bus. They waved from the windows and then the bus pulled away, turning a corner at the end of the street, and heading back to the open road.

Spitz led Ray to the railyards, and they overnighted in an empty boxcar. The boxcar smelled vaguely of coal dust and wheat chaff. The floorboards were gnarled and twisted, and an errant nail poked into Spitz's spine as he tried to sleep. Ray sat up into the night, blowing his harmonica, and that gave Spitz some pleasure. He nodded off as Ray was playing a jaunty tune called "Shine on Harvest Moon."

When Spitz awoke the next morning, the train was moving, clattering along the tracks with a rising tempo. He stood up precariously and walked, with his feet a yard apart, to the open door of the boxcar. America went gliding by in a pastiche of greens and browns. There were mountains and rivers and canyons and creeks and brawling cities and one-horse towns, and Spitz felt in his bones that one day the land would be healthy again. Ray was propped up in a corner, sleeping the Depression away as though it were a bad dream.

In boxcars and on top of them, sometimes alone and sometimes in the company of other world-weary men, they traversed the countryside. San Francisco crept up on them in the middle of the night, and they disembarked from the train. A dutiful policeman found them, slumbering on sturdy benches in the waiting room of the station, and he escorted them out of the trainyard. They walked through the hilly streets, past Chinese restaurants and lobster huts, and dipped their feet in the healing ocean.

On a street called Haight, they walked past bars and ancient houses. They noticed a commotion down one of the back alleys. Two burly thugs were beating up on a smaller Black man. They had him down, stomping at his head and torso. It didn't seem fair. Spitz stopped at the mouth of the alley and hollered at the men. "Hey, stop that!"

The thugs turned to look at him. The meanness in their faces was irrational, anything but human. "You want some of this?" one of them said. His voice sounded like the growl of a dog.

"I want you to stop," Spitz said, "before someone gets hurt."

As the two thugs approached him, Spitz reached into his duffle bag and produced a thirty-five-inch piece of hickory. The second thug grinned menacingly. "Whatcha gonna do with that?"

"You'll see, I guess."

The thugs kept coming. Spitz cocked the bat and hit one of them on the shin. The man dropped to his knees and fell backwards, clutching his leg and moaning. The second thug collected a blow along the side of his head that sent him reeling. The first guy found his feet and approached again. Spitz cocked the bat and swung. He could hear ribs breaking, and the man belched like a gut-shot cow and dropped to his knees. Spitz kicked him in the teeth. He stood above the two goons, when the fight had gone out of them, with his bat at the ready. "Are ya done?"

"Yeah, we're done," the first thug said, breathing heavy.

"Then disappear."

The thug staggered to his feet and helped his buddy off the cobblestones. The two of them limped out of the alley.

Spitz gave his bat to Ray and walked toward the Black man, who was sitting near a trash can, dazed and bloody. He was not a young man. His nose looked broken, and there was a gash on his forehead that would need stitches. Spitz didn't recognize him at first. "You okay?" he asked.

"I've had better days," the man muttered through broken teeth.

"What gripe did those guys have with you?"

"Didn't appreciate my routine, I guess." The old man stared at Spitz for a long time, and then he peered down the alley at Ray. "Are you the same fellas?" he asked. "The ones I met back in St. Louis, couple months ago?"

Spitz knelt and observed the man more closely. "You're the dancer."

"I can dance a lick now and then."

"And your name was—"

"Bojangles." The old man didn't try to stand, and Spitz thought it best to let him rest a while. "So tell me," Bojangles said, "did your odyssey go as I predicted?"

Spitz smiled at him. "It ain't over yet."

Bojangles' face contorted into a kind of grin. "I'm sure you'll do very well."

"I live in hope," Spitz said.

The old man nodded at Ray. "And the boy is goin home at last?"

"He is."

"Good."

Spitz looked around the sunlit alley. "Say, where's your dog?"

Bojangles whimpered softly. It was the first sign of self-pity Spitz had seen in him. "The dog up and died three weeks ago now."

"I'm sorry."

"So am I."

"Are you gonna be all right?" Spitz asked.

"I'll be right as rain in a day or two," the old man said. "Just help me to my feet." Spitz grasped the old man's elbow and hoisted him gently to a standing position. It wasn't difficult. Bojangles was nothing but skin and bones. Placing one of the old man's arms over his shoulder, Spitz walked him out to the street. They found a large brick house, and Spitz sat the old man down to rest again on the cement front steps. "Just leave me here," Bojangles said. "I'll be safe right here."

"Are you sure?

"And thank you for steppin in back there. You're an upright fella."

"It wasn't anything."

"You are indeed a Samaritan. And a good one."

"We'll take our leave then," Spitz said. "I hope we'll meet again."

"Nothin's ever final," Bojangles said. "Some people are on the road, but I think you are on your way."

"On my way to what?"

"To whatever you're lookin for."

On a gravel highway south of the city, Spitz held out his thumb until a Mexican worker in an empty fruit truck stopped to pick them up. "Where jou heading?" the Mexican asked, as Spitz helped Ray into the box of the truck.

"Salinas."

"Ees on my way," the man said, and then he threw the truck into gear.

Red dust in their eyes and in their mouths, they rode past orchards and vineyards, on mountain roads and flats. They saw giant redwoods and stately pines. At the edge of Salinas, dirty and tired, they clambered out of the box of the truck and thanked the driver for the ride. As they walked down an approach and into town, Ray became more cognizant of his surroundings. "This place looks familiar," he said.

"It ought to," Spitz replied. "You were born here."

"I was born here?"

"Yeah."

They walked into the town in the heat of the afternoon and knocked on the flimsy screen door of the first house that looked inhabited. There was no answer. They knocked again. After a moment, an unshaven man, wearing a ragged pair of dungarees and nothing else, appeared on the other side of the screen. He was skinny and hard, and a hand-rolled cigarette dangled from his lips like it was a permanent fixture. Spitz could see ink stains on his hands, deep and blue and etched into his skin like tattoos. The man stared hard at them as if they were evangelicals. "I don't want what you're selling."

"We ain't sellin nothin."

He took a drag on his cigarette. "Then what do you want?"

"We were just wondering," Spitz said quickly, before the man had a chance to turn away, "if you could tell us where Lincoln Avenue is. John Chatterwood's place?"

The unshaven man looked at Spitz like he was two bricks short of a load. "Professor Chatterwood's gone. We lost him two years ago."

Spitz was thrown for a loop, but he had the presence of mind to ask, "Is his wife still alive?"

"She is," the man said, pointing south down the street. "Big white house, past the Town Hall."

"Well, thank you."

As Spitz was turning to leave, the unshaven man spoke up again. "You're that ball player," he said. "Spitball McKague."

"Yeah, I am." Spitz wondered what this admission might cost him in Ray's hometown.

"Your picture was in all the papers a couple of years back."

"Well, we've gotta be goin."

"Sorry I was a little abrupt when you first came to the door," the man said. "I was in the middle of writing some purple prose."

"Are you a writer?"

"Yeah."

"Seem to be a lot of 'em around these days," Spitz said.

"I want to write something about a baseball player." The man was a tad-bit friendlier now. "Do you think you could sit and talk with me sometime?"

"Sure," Spitz replied, "right after we visit Missus Chatterwood."

It seemed like a long walk to the big white house on Lincoln. On the way, Spitz rehearsed in his head all the things he might say to Ray's mother. None of them sounded good enough. Ray was unusually quiet. They passed the school grounds and a baseball diamond, brown clumpy grass and red clay, a mound eaten away by years of erosion. Ray lingered near the edge of the diamond. "I remember this place," he said. He pointed to a grey wooden grandstand. "I remember my daddy sittin right there."

"You were a goddamn good third baseman," Spitz told him. "One of the best I ever seen."

"Was I good?" Ray looked at him with wide eyes.

"One of the best."

They proceeded through the downtown with its pool halls and its five-and-dimes, past a sporting goods store, now closed, where Ray had probably gotten his first baseball glove. At last, Spitz saw the Town Hall and a residential street just beyond it and a white house on that street. Spitz found the calling card in the pocket of his jeans and looked at it. The number on the house was the same as the number on the card. The house was two and a half stories, the granddam of an earlier era, but it was now unpainted and in bad need of shingles. "That's my house!" Ray exclaimed, about ready to break into a run.

"Hold on," Spitz said. He grabbed Ray by the shoulders and looked him in the eye. They stood on the sidewalk in front of the large open veranda for a moment while Spitz collected himself. "There's something I gotta tell ya," he said. "Yer daddy might not live here no more."

"Might not live here?"

"No."

"He's gone? Like the man said?"

Spitz couldn't find an answer.

Together they climbed the rickety front step. Spitz took a breath to calm himself and knocked on the door. Then he went back down to the sidewalk, leaving Ray on the veranda. After a moment, a lady opened the door. She was smart-looking, in a brown house dress, with her grey hair done up in curls.

"Momma," Ray said. The lady looked at him in disbelief, almost as if she didn't recognize her own son. But then she did. She clutched him in her arms like only a mother could. She was weeping. "Don't cry, Momma."

The lady wept a good long time. She didn't seem to notice Spitz, standing on the sidewalk near the front step. She held her son as though he were a new-born child. "You've been away these five years," she whispered, "and in that time, your papa—"

"I know." Ray looked at her blankly, like the full impact of the realization hadn't touched him yet. "I heard a man talkin."

Getting control of herself at last, she examined Ray's childlike face, brushing a lock of hair out of his eyes. "Supper's almost ready," she said. "You go on inside now and wash up."

"I will," Ray said. He disappeared into the house.

The lady looked full-on at Spitz for the first time. Her gaze was not particularly cheerful. "You brought him home," she said in an even voice.

"I'm the one who hit him with that pitch," Spitz said.

"I know," she said. "I've seen your photograph."

"I didn't mean to. The ball got away on me."

She glared at Spitz. "He was a vibrant young man."

"He was."

"And you ended that."

Spitz stood there, at a loss for words. He could think of nothing else to say that would make things right.

"At least you faced up to it," the lady said. "That's a start." She came down the step toward him. "I've thought about this moment for a long time. I thought, if I ever saw you, I'd slap your face for what you've done."

"I wouldn't blame you, ma'am."

"But now I see that you've been hurt by it too."

"I'm sorry," Spitz said. His tears came from somewhere deep in his belly, in waves, and shook him to the core. The tears were fierce and tender. The lady reached out and enfolded him in her arms and, for a moment, she was his mother too.

They all had supper afterwards in a dining room that looked like it was built for Christmas dinners. There was artwork on the oak paneled walls, paintings of seascapes and broad sunlit beaches. Against one wall stood a large china cabinet, filled to the brim with ornate dishes and family photographs. There were several pictures of Ray at various stages in his childhood and in his baseball career. Spitz particularly liked a photo of Ray in his Pacific Coast League days, looking like a younger, handsomer Shoeless Joe Jackson as he chased down a flyball. There was a wedding picture from the early 1900s, and a picture of Ray's father with a book in his hand underneath a leafy tree. He was dressed in a white suit. He resembled Mark Twain, thought Spitz, with his handlebar moustache and long white hair.

The supper was a simple stew, the kind a woman might cook if she was expecting to eat alone. Spitz had eaten better suppers in his life but, when he was finished and Ray's mother was out of the room finding a jar of canned fruit, he hid two crisp ten-dollar bills under his plate. "I'm gonna go now," he told Ray.

"Aw Spitzy," Ray said, "ain't you gonna stay with us?"

"I can't."

"We got an extra room upstairs."

"You'll be fine without me," Spitz said.

"I could hit you fungo every day."

"Maybe someday we'll play together again."

Ray looked at him earnestly. "People always say *someday* when they mean *never*."

"I gotta go find my own way home."

Ray smiled and touched Spitz's sleeve. "Have you got a daddy?"

"Yeah."

"I guess you do gotta go home then."

Spitz pushed his chair back and stood up. "I'm gonna miss you, Ray."

"I'm gonna miss you too, Spitzy. I'll think of you when I'm playin my mouth harp."

"You do that."

Out in the kitchen, Spitz thanked Ray's mother for the supper. "I hope you can forgive me one day," he said.

Ray's mother was ladling canned peaches into a large bowl. She stopped and glanced up at him. Her eyes were dull and sad. "I forgive you already," she said. "I should have done that long ago."

When Spitz walked out of the Chatterwood's house that evening, he felt like a two-ton weight had been lifted off his shoulders. He breathed in the warmth of the August evening and looked up at the stately turret on the Town Hall. Then he marched down the street toward the writer's bungalow, hoping to keep the only promise he'd ever made in Salinas.

A month later, Spitz clambered out of the box of a half-ton truck and stood on the side of a dirt road in the Smoky Mountains of Georgia. Duffle bag slung over his shoulder, he gazed through the fog at the wood-frame house in the clearing. It was early in the day. The rooster in the farmyard had not yet announced the rise of the sun. The old hound on the front porch, still sleeping, had not picked up Spitz's scent. Setting his duffle on the side of the road, Spitz stood and watched the squat house until Gwendolyn appeared on the front stoop.

She was wearing a grey gingham dress. Spitz remembered her wearing that same dress five years earlier. It was newer then, not so faded and ragged at the seams. But the girl inside the dress was neither faded nor ragged. The intervening years had brought her into focus. Her face was thinner now but still beautiful. Her hair, no longer in a ponytail, was still blonde.

Her shoulders and arms were more slender and somehow more graceful as she strode out into the greenness of the yard. Spitz watched as she primed the pump and then filled a tin pail with water. She did not observe Spitz observing her.

Then the door of the house flew open, and a young boy catapulted himself off the step, running toward Gwendolyn. He was a handsome lad, bare-footed, in dungarees and a torn shirt. The child pointed a wooden pistol at Gwendolyn and pretended to fire. "Cue! Cue! Cue!" he shouted. Gwendolyn laughed and feigned a wound. Watching the boy and his mother, Spitz was wounded for real. His knees wanted to buckle. He felt resentment and remorse, but mostly he felt sorry for himself.

The dog woke up. Sensing a stranger, the old mutt sauntered off the porch and barked, hollow and cowardly, in Spitz's direction. Gwendolyn turned and looked. She didn't seem to recognize Spitz at first. She stood there, looking at him for a long time. The boy looked at him too. Spitz froze, and they stood there, in that tableau, for what seemed like an eternity, Gwendolyn with her hand still on the pump, the boy squinting into the sun as the fog lifted, Spitz with his arms at his sides. Only the dog made a sound, and his barking cracked the stillness of the mountain morning.

When the dog had finished with his empty remonstrations, Gwendolyn spoke. "Tom?" she said. "Is that you?"

"I told you I'd come back."

"It's been so long."

Spitz walked up the driveway toward her. The dog growled at him. "You have a son?"

"Yes?"

"I s'pose I should have expected something like that."

"Why didn't you write?"

"I couldn't."

"Why didn't you answer my letters?"

"I was ashamed."

Gwendolyn left the pail sitting by the pump and took her young son by the hand. "I think you'd better go."

Spitz couldn't think of anything else to say. His heart raced, and he was tongue-tied like a kid who has been forced to read out loud in public for the first time. Gwendolyn marched past him, child in tow, climbed the steps and went inside the house. The screen door slammed shut behind her. The hound growled. Spitz stared him down. The hound cowered, slunk back up on the porch and whimpered. Spitz trudged out to the road again, picking up his duffle bag and slinging it over his shoulder. He did not know what to do next. He looked at the pocket watch Gwendolyn had given him. It was ticking again. He thought to head back down toward the main highway, and he was just about to do that when he heard the door of the house creak open again. Gwendolyn's papa stepped outside, an old gentleman with his hair cropped short and the skinny body of a man who'd spent his life in the mines. "Tom!" he hollered. "Tom? Is that you?"

"It's me," Spitz hollered back.

"Git back here then!"

Spitz hesitated and then walked back up the driveway. Gwendolyn's father met him halfway. He meant business. "You treated my daughter like trash," he said.

"I didn't mean to, sir."

"You can't blame her fer bein angry."

"No sir, I don't."

The old man's eyes were blazing. "Do you love her?"

"I do."

"Then you got to give her time."

"Time?" Spitz said. "She has a family of her own now."

Gwendolyn's father horked on the gravel. "Did you happen to git a good look at the boy?"

"Not up close."

"Well, if you looked at him, you'd see that he has the same eyes as you." The old man's jaw was set, like he was chipping away at a piece of granite with a pickaxe. "Are you gonna make an honest woman of my daughter or ain't ya?"

A hundred emotions flooded in. Spitz felt them in the pit of his stomach and in his chest and throat. Guilt and anger found a home there but also love and a sense of wonder. And if others could forgive him, could he not forgive himself? He straightened up and looked Gwendolyn's father in the eye. "I will if she'll have me."

"Oh, she'll have you," the old man said. "I'll see to that. Now you'd best come on inside."

Gwendolyn's father turned and went back to the house. Spitz saw Gwendolyn, framed in the kitchen window, the boy in her arms. He crossed the yard toward her, toward the light that was in her eyes.

The sun was rising high over the Smoky Mountains, burning off the last of the morning fog. The heavy scent of goldenrod, in its last dog days of fall, was everywhere, and there was freshness in the moss and the crisp, dry leaves. Robins were trilling in the branches of the yellow birch trees. The grass was as green as Spitz remembered it, the sky above him impossibly blue, and he could almost taste the delicate sweetness of the still mountain air.

About the Author

Dwayne Brenna is the award-winning author of several books of humor, poetry, and fiction. Coteau Books published his popular series of humorous vignettes entitled *Eddie Gustafson's Guide to Christmas* in 2000. His two books of poetry, *Stealing Home* and *Give My Love to Rose*, were published by Hagios Press in 2012 and 2015 respectively. *Stealing Home*, a poetic celebration of the game of baseball, was subsequently shortlisted for several Saskatchewan Book Awards, including the University of Regina Book of the Year Award. His first novel *New Albion*, about a laudanum-addicted playwright struggling to survive in London's East End during the winter of 1850-51, was published by Coteau Books in autumn 2016. *New Albion* won the 2017 Muslims for Peace and Justice Fiction Award at the Saskatchewan Book Awards. It was one of three English language novels shortlisted for the prestigious MM Bennetts Award for historical fiction. His short stories and poems have been published in an array of journals, including *Grain*, *Nine*, *Spitball*, *Intima*, *The Cold Mountain Review*, and *The Antigonish Review*.

Manufactured by Amazon.ca
Bolton, ON